THE WEREWOLF MASK

by
Kenneth Ireland

ℛR
RAVETTE PUBLISHING

© 2001 Kenneth Ireland
All rights reserved.

First published by Ravette Publishing 2001

This book is sold subject to the condition that it
shall not, by way of trade or otherwise, be lent,
resold, hired out or otherwise circulated without the
publisher's prior consent in any form of binding or
cover other than that in which it is published and
without a similar condition including this condition
being imposed on the subsequent purchaser.

Printed and bound in Great Britain
for Ravette Publishing Limited,
Unit 3, Tristar Centre,
Star Road, Partridge Green,
West Sussex RH13 8RA
by Cox & Wyman Ltd, Reading, Berkshire

ISBN: 1 84161 033 X

CONTENTS

THE WEREWOLF MASK

The mask looked just like a horrible werewolf with blood dripping from its fangs. It was one which fitted right over Peter's head, with spaces for his eyes so that when he looked out the movements gave an extra dimension of horror to the already terrifying expression.

The hair hanging down from the top of the mask looked real, as did the hair and whiskers dropping from the sides and face. Peter felt it was very satisfying, as soon as he had been into the joke shop and bought it.

Something, however, was missing. While the mask seemed realistic enough, it was his hands which were wrong. If a human could really turn into a werewolf, it would not only be the face which could change, but hands would grow hairy as well.

He discovered this when he unwrapped the paper bag in which he had bought the mask and went upstairs to try the effect in front of his dressing table mirror. As long as he kept his hands hidden all was well, but once his hands were seen, they were far too smooth. In fact they weren't hairy at all. It was rather disappointing, but even so he thought he'd try out the effect anyway.

His mother was in, so making grunting and drooling noises he loped his way down the stairs. He went into the living room where his mother was darning some socks, flung open the door and leaped in, arms raised to his shoulders, fingers extended like claws, and growling ferociously.

"My goodness," said his mother, looking up. "What on earth made you waste your money on a thing like that?"

"I thought it looked cool," said Peter, not at all put out. "Doesn't it look – well, real?"

"Well, it was your birthday money, so I suppose you could spend it how you liked," said his mother placidly, returning to the socks. "I don't know how you manage to get such large holes in these, I really don't. I think it must be the way you yank them on."

"But doesn't it look just like a werewolf?" asked Peter, taking the mask off and examining it carefully.

"It would, I suppose, except there are no such things and never have been such things as werewolves. I think you've wasted your money on something of no real use," his mother replied. "It would have been better spent on some new socks. Still, your Aunty Doreen did tell you to spend it on something to amuse you, so I suppose we can't expect anything else."

"The thing that's wrong with it is my hands," said Peter. "The face is all right, but the hands are wrong. Don't you think?"

He put the mask on again and held out his hands for her to see. She glanced at him briefly.

"Putting a mask on like that won't make your hands look different from a boy's," she said. "The only thing you could do is wear gloves, your woolly ones perhaps, to disguise them."

Since she was taking no more notice of him, he went back upstairs, drew a pair of woolly gloves from a drawer in his dressing table, and tried the effect this time. Well, perhaps it wasn't all that bad. At least the gloves gave some kind of appearance of hairiness, but it was still not quite right.

He tried combing the backs of the gloves, but that was no good. When he tried the claw effect, it wasn't half as good as when his nails were showing.

He still had some money left, so he

went back to the joke shop, taking the mask with him.

"Have you got anything like hairy hands?" he asked.

The shopkeeper, being a bit of a joker himself, looked at his own hands and asked if they would do. Then he looked down at his feet behind the counter and, as if in surprise, announced that he hadn't got pigs' trotters either.

"No. I mean," explained Peter, carefully, "I bought this werewolf mask and I wondered if you had a kind of hairy hand to go with it. You know, to make the whole thing look – well, more real."

"Hairy, with sort of claws, you mean?" asked the shopkeeper, nodding. "I might have. Hang on."

He went along the shelves behind the counter, opened first one drawer, then another and, at the third drawer, extracted a transparent plastic bag which he placed on the counter.

"These do?" he asked.

Peter picked it up eagerly and inspected the contents through the plastic. They seemed about right to him.

"Can I try them on?" he asked.

"Sure." The shopkeeper ripped open the bag and laid the hands out for him.

They weren't like gloves because they didn't cover the hands all round, but merely lay on top and were fastened by a strap underneath and another round the wrist. Just the tips of the fingers fitted into sockets so the rubber fingers would not dangle about uselessly.

"You can't expect a perfect fit," the shopkeeper said, "because they don't make them in different sizes. If they're too big, just tighten the strap underneath and pull the one that goes round your wrist up a bit."

He helped him put them on. They were rather big, but with them pushed well up his hands and over his wrists, they were not at all bad. Peter decided he would have them, if he could afford them.

They were just as good as the magnificent mask, with what looked like real hair growing along the backs, really satisfying long claws with just enough red on the ends to look as if they had torn into somebody's flesh. What was more, the red was actually painted to look as if it was still wet.

"Try the effect of both the mask and the hands," suggested the shopkeeper, pointing to a mirror on the wall behind the door. So Peter did. That was much better, especially in the fairly dim light inside the shop. Absolutely terrifying, almost!

"Wrap them up for you?" asked the shopkeeper.

"No, I'll take them as they are," said

Peter.

"Pardon?" said the shopkeeper. The mask was not adjusted correctly, so his voice had been rather muffled.

Peter straightened the mask round his face so that his mouth was in the right place. "No thanks. How much?"

He paid the money and left the shop wearing his new purchases. He just happened to have noticed Billy Fidler leaning against the post box outside, looking the other way.

He ran out of the shop, crept round the side of the postbox then slowly reached out a hand to touch Billy on the shoulder. Billy turned, as he expected him to do.

"That's pretty good," said Billy, standing up. "I like the hands." Then he peered closer. "Hi, Peter."

"What do you think of it, then?" asked Peter.

"Pretty good. I could only really tell who you were by the clothes. It needs to be darker, though. I mean, you don't expect to come across a werewolf in daylight, so it just looks like a horrible mask and a pair of hands right now. If it was dark, though, and you suddenly came at me, that would really give me a nasty turn. Can I try them on?"

Peter didn't mind, and in any case he wanted to find out if what Billy had said was true. When Billy put them on, he found it was. They were very good indeed. Very effective for what they were. Money well spent. Although it was true that in broad daylight, on the pavement, outside a row of shops, with a post box just next to them, the mask was just a mask and the hands obviously artificial.

"Try them out on her," said Peter, seeing Wendy Glover approaching with her mother. She was a girl at their school who always seemed to frighten quite easily.

Billy obediently popped behind the post box. As Wendy and her mother drew level, he suddenly jumped out in front of them. Wendy's mother drew her daughter a little closer to her with disdain.

"Billy Fidler, I should think," remarked Wendy primly to her mother as they continued along the pavement. She turned after they had walked on a few paces. "A bit silly, I think," she called, loudly.

"I tell you, it would be a different story if it was dark," said Billy firmly, taking the mask and the hands off again and giving them back to Peter. "You try it, and see if I'm not right."

Peter slipped them into his pockets and went home, taking them upstairs and placing them carefully in the drawer of his dressing table. He tried not to fold them and make any creases in them.

It began to get dark quite early that

evening. So, at the first opportunity, Peter slipped upstairs, stood in front of the mirror and tried the mask on again without switching on his bedroom light. When he strapped the werewolf hands on to his own and tried out the effect, he almost managed to frighten himself, it looked so real!

Then he knew what was lacking, and ran downstairs into the kitchen, hurrying back up to his bedroom with a little pocket torch in his hands. This time, he drew the curtains as well, and when the room was pitch black, held the torch just underneath his chin and switched it on suddenly.

This time he really did jump in fright! In front of him was a monster, really horrible, writhing and drooling with just a hint of blood on the tips of its fangs. From its claws more blood shone in the light as if freshly drawn from a victim.

He moved his left hand across his mouth as though trying to wipe it clean. It was so realistic that he was glad to know that downstairs both of his parents were in the house.

"Well, well," he said aloud, very pleased with himself, and hurried to switch on the light.

He put out the torch, sat on his bed and watched himself in the mirror as he removed first the hands and then the mask. It was almost a relief to be able to see himself return to normal again. The only thing was, when would he ever have the opportunity to try these things out properly?

His father was calling from downstairs.

"Peter!"

"What?"

"Come down and I'll tell you."

Peter was about to replace his toys in the drawer again when he thought better of it and stuffed them into his pockets instead, along with the torch. If his father wanted him to go out, this might be just the chance he had been hoping for.

He went downstairs to find his father waiting for him in the hall.

"I've just remembered a couple of errands I'd like doing. You know the envelopes I've been putting through people's doors, collecting for the children's hospital?"

"Yes." Good! His father did want him to go out, then.

"There are two houses I called to collect them from last night, but the occupants were out. Just those two. Would you mind popping round to see if they're in tonight and collect them if they are? Take this with you." He handed over a little identity card to say that his father was an authorised collector. "And explain who you are. They'll know you anyway, I expect, but take it just in case."

"Which houses are they?"

"Number eighteen, along our road, Mr and Mrs Hubbard. Then number forty-seven, Devonshire Road. He's new, so I don't know his name."

"No trouble," said Peter. "Won't take me ten minutes, Dad."

"Okay then. Remember it's the children's hospital envelopes you're asking for," his father called after him.

"I know," said Peter, hurrying away.

Once he was clear of the house, he carefully took the mask out of his pocket and put it on, then the hands. Now with the little torch held ready, he set off along the street.

Number eighteen was not far away, but as he walked towards it Peter realised that there was nobody out on the street but himself. It was nicely dark by now, and the sky was clouded over, but all at once a cloud slid to one side and he saw that somewhere up there was not only the moon, but a full one at that. Just the right sort of night for a werewolf to be abroad, he thought, as the cloud glided back into place again.

He adjusted the mask so that the eyes and the mouth were in the right places, and pulled up the hairy hands as far as they would go. Then he continued briskly towards number eighteen where he knocked on the door.

For a while there was no answer. Then

he heard the chain behind the door rattle, then a pause.

"Who is it?" he heard a woman's voice ask from inside.

"I've come for the envelope for the children's hospital," he said loudly.

"Just a minute."

There was another pause, and he assumed that Mrs Hubbard was trying to find it so she could put some money inside before opening the door. He got ready. Then the chain rattled a second time, and the door opened. As the figure of Mrs Hubbard appeared, he switched the torch on, directly under his chin.

Mrs Hubbard started, and stepped back. Peter stood motionless with the light unwavering underneath his chin. There was a gasp, Mrs Hubbard clutched at her chest, then the door slammed shut and he heard the chain rattle again and then a bolt clunk into place.

That was great, Peter decided. He did think of knocking on the door again, this time with his mask off, but thought better of it. She might not come to the door twice. Now for whoever it was who lived at number forty-seven Devonshire Road.

This was a large, gloomy house, with some kind of tall fir trees growing in the front garden behind a thick hedge. He didn't remember ever having visited this house before. He opened the wooden gate and walked up the path. He found the front door was not at the front of the house, but at the side, with more thick hedge growing in front of it on the opposite side of the narrow path. He wondered how anyone managed to carry furniture into the house when the path was as narrow as that.

He had no need to flash his torch at the doorbell, because it was one of those illuminated ones, with a name on a card underneath it. *Luke Anthrope*, it said. So that was the name of the man who lived there. What an unusual name! He pressed the bell and at once heard an angry buzzing noise from somewhere inside, not like a bell at all.

There was no answer. Feeling safe and secure behind his mask, he pressed the button again. This time he heard a man's voice from inside the hall of this dark house, which rather surprised him, since there were no lights switched on that he could see.

"Go round the back," it said hoarsely.

He walked further along the path to find a tall wooden gate, which opened easily. He passed through it, saw the back door of the house and knocked on it. The door opened just as the moon came out again, but he was ready for it and had the torch under his chin immediately.

Mr Anthrope did not frighten easily, however. He was a short man, with a thick beard and moustache, and he just stood there regarding Peter steadily.

"I've come for the envelope for the children's hospital," said Peter, switching his torch off since it was obviously having no effect.

"Ah, yes," said Mr Anthrope, but made no move to go and fetch it.

"I've got a card here," said Peter, fumbling in his pocket with some difficulty since the hairy gloves got in the way. "It's my father's really, but it proves you can give the envelope to me."

The short man continued to regard him without moving.

"Switch that torch on again," he said. So Peter did.

"Do you know why you never see two robins on a Christmas card?" the man asked him suddenly.

Peter did not.

"It's because if you ever find two robins together, they fight each other to the death. Did you know that? You only find one robin in one place at a time. The same with one or two other creatures."

Peter had no idea what this Mr Anthrope was on about. He had not mentioned robins. Robins had nothing to do with it, and, what other creatures?

The man's face was beginning to change rather strangely in the moonlight, which was now shining full upon him. It was as if his beard was growing more straggly, somehow, and the face becoming more lined. Also, his lips seemed to be thinner and more drawn back over his teeth. Peter noticed, too, now that the light was brighter, how hairy this man's hands were. Peter turned off the torch, because he didn't need it now.

Then Mr Anthrope did a very strange thing. He came right out to the edge of his doorstep and leaned towards Peter as if he was going to whisper something to him.

Mr Anthrope's mouth was somewhere near his ear. Peter, always curious, strained to be able to hear what Mr Anthrope was about to whisper to him. He was astonished then to feel the bones in the side of his neck crunching, and blood running down inside his shirt. He didn't even have time to cry out before long nails were tearing at his flesh.

THE GIRL WHO READ TOO MUCH

Lorinda hated her grandmother, and that was all there was to it! Grandmother had brought her up since she was quite small. Perhaps that was not quite true, Lorinda decided. Her grandmother had hardly brought her up at all. Her bringing-up had been left to a series of nannies and servants. Grandmother was always too busy going about her own affairs and was away from the house almost as much as she was there. A very busy social life, had granny.

For granny was very rich, and they lived in a large house. There was the chauffeur-handyman, the cook who was his wife, a part-time gardener and a maid. There were two things wrong, however. First, Granny was rich only because Lorinda's parents had been rich before they had died.

Their money should have gone to Lorinda. Not to her.

Secondly, if granny should die, Lorinda was the only relative and she would receive all that money and be rich herself. But Lorinda was only twelve, and granny was not elderly. She was not even sixty yet and might live for another twenty or thirty years. That was a long time to wait before Lorinda would be able to do just as she liked.

In the meantime, it seemed almost as if granny resented her for being there at all. For the slightest thing she would punish Lorinda quite severely. Like the time when Lorinda had decided that the cook's food was uneatable and had taken it back to the kitchen and emptied her plate over the floor. On that occasion, granny had sent her to her room immediately and had kept her there all night.

When Lorinda had cut the whiskers off the cat to see if what she had read was true (that without them a cat could no longer pass through small holes), granny had actually smacked her. When Lorinda had been sick in the hall of the large house where they lived, and had covered it with a copy of that morning's newspaper instead of telling the maid, granny had been so cross it was quite amusing to think about it afterwards.

Lorinda, not having many friends, spent a great deal of her time reading, usually up in her room. Living in such a large house, meant she did not have many friends because they felt out of place there, so Lorinda had to find her own entertainment.

In the meantime, her hatred of her grandmother grew steadily. Lucinda decided it was time to find out whether or not something could be done to put matters right.

Normally Lorinda read story books, but one day she found a book on the shelves, in what used to be her father's study, called *The Complete Guide to the Law*. She thought it might be interesting and turned to the section headed *Children and the Law*, where she discovered some fascinating information!

A child under the age of ten could not be convicted of any crime at all. So if she was, say, only nine, she could kill her grandmother and get away with it. Unfortunately, she was twelve. Between the ages of ten and fourteen, she read, a child could only be convicted of a crime if it could be proved that the child knew that he or she had done wrong. Now how could anyone prove that?

It was the last item which held Lucinda's attention. Up to the age of seventeen, no matter what a child did, the maximum penalty was only a fine of a few hundred pounds or a period in a young offenders institution.

She considered the possibilities. Suppose she did get rid of her grandmother and had to pay a fine. As she would inherit all of the money when her grandmother died, the fine wouldn't seem a great deal to pay. Alternatively, she might be sent to a young offenders institution. The book didn't mention for how long. Well, even if it was for a few years, it could still be worth it.

Now were there any snags? She looked up *Inheritance*. There was nothing there about not being able to inherit the money which was rightly hers anyway, so that was all right. Then Lorinda thought a little harder. She had read in the newspapers about murderers who had pleaded insanity and got away with it. Supposing she killed granny – would it be possible to claim she had been insane at the time?

She looked that up, too, but was not pleased with what she found there. If she were able to prove that she was insane, she might find herself locked away in a special home for a very long time indeed, and that would be no good at all!

No, she had better not be insane. In any case, she was not insane in the slightest, she was quite certain of that. You could not be insane and intelligent at the same time, could you? So she might as well start planning anyway. If somehow anyone could prove later that she had known the difference between right and wrong – which would be difficult – she might find herself locked up for a year or two.

It would be well worth it, she decided. All the money would be hers, there would be no harsh interfering grandmother, and she would be able to do as she liked at last. Of course, it would be best not to get caught in the first place.

She read a couple of murder mysteries while she thought more about it.

The stairway in the house was made of marble. Because the stairs were so beautiful and quite a feature of the house, no stair carpet was laid. With their heavy brass balustrade and ornately-carved wooden handrails, they were very impressive. They led up to a balcony running round the hall, from which other doors led.

Every morning, her grandmother would work in her own study upstairs, dealing with correspondence. Then, when the gong sounded for lunch, she would walk down the stairs to the dining room. Lorinda was often downstairs by that time when she was not at school.

Lorinda went out to take a careful look at these stairs. Supposing someone actually tripped somewhere near the top! They would almost certainly fall headlong – to the bottom. If they hit their head on the edge of one of those hard marble stairs, or better still, collided with one of the two solid posts at the bottom, they would be dead for certain!

She waited for her chance. Then, when the cook was somewhere else for a moment and her grandmother was still upstairs, Lorinda nipped into the kitchen, sneaked out with a packet of lard and rubbed it on the third, fourth and fifth stairs from the top ...

Better not rub it on the very top step, she thought, because there was just a chance her grandmother might notice it glistening there. By rubbing it on the lower steps she would suspect nothing. Then she waited quietly until the gong sounded.

At once granny appeared from her room and started down the stairs, slipped and fell headlong – just as Lorinda began to cross the hall into the dining room.

Granny was very cross indeed as she picked herself up and rubbed a bruise on her left elbow.

"I might have been killed," she said to Lorinda, angrily. "Mason! Where are you?"

At once the maid came running, in answer to her shout.

"Mason, those stairs are very slippery. I want them scrubbed clean at once. I don't know how they have become so slippery, but if it happens again you will be dismissed instantly."

And, still rubbing her bruise, she limped into the dining room.

Obviously murder was not so simple, especially if you were going to do it with the least risk of being detected. Lorinda, while quite willing to spend a little time in a young offenders institution, would rather not if it could be avoided. It might not be very comfortable living in one of those places.

Now what was that she'd read about ten-year-olds? Under the age of ten, no child could be convicted of any crime. Supposing she could persuade a nine-year-old to kill granny for her? That would save her the trouble of doing it herself, and the child couldn't be convicted at all.

The problem was, which nine-year-old, and how to get him to do it without arousing suspicion? It had to be a boy, she decided, because girls of that age might not be so inclined towards adventure.

She walked down the long drive to the pavement while she thought about it and looked around to see if there was a suitable nine-year-old boy available for her purposes. Soon, a small boy on a rather large bicycle rode towards her along the pavement. She looked him over casually.

"Hello," she said smiling sweetly.

The boy stopped.

"Hi!" he said.

"How old are you?" she asked.

25

"I'm nine. Why?"

At that moment her grandmother came up behind her, walking through the gates.

"Lorinda, I'm catching a bus into town," she announced.

"What's wrong with the car?" asked Lorinda in surprise. This actually gave her another idea. She could fix the car brakes so the car crashed and killed everyone inside.

However, she dismissed that idea at once, as she had no idea how to fix a car's brakes. And in any case Davies, the chauffeur, always drove so slowly that even if the brakes did fail there wouldn't be much more than a gentle bump!

"It's Davies's afternoon off. I can't get a taxi in time so I shall use public transport," said her grandmother. "Behave yourself while I'm gone." And she walked, still limping a little, to the bus stop.

The traffic was rather busy at this time of day. In fact the cars hurtled past as the road was absolutely straight at that point. A bus came up, but her grandmother stood back because it had the wrong number on the front. The bus pulled right into the kerb, stopped quickly, a few passengers got off, and then it drove away again.

Now Lorinda could hardly push her grandmother under a bus, effective though that might be. On the other hand ...

"That's not your mother, is it?" the boy was asking.

"No – my grandmother," she replied. Then she looked carefully at him and his bike. He didn't look very bright. Perhaps he would be just right for what she had in mind.

"She likes a joke," she said. "Do you feel like playing a trick on her?"

"If you like," said the boy, gleefully.

"I'll give you fifty pence," said Lorinda, "if you could ride up behind her, as if you're going to run her over, and make her jump!"

"All right," said the boy. "Anything for a laugh."

"Well, when I tell you, ride up close behind her, then shout and see if she jumps. You'd better keep away from the edge of the pavement, though, in case you fall off into the road. You don't want to get run over."

"What if *she* gets run over?" asked the boy. Obviously he was not quite as simple as he seemed.

"She won't," Lorinda laughed. "She just jumps straight up into the air and down again. She always does."

A second bus was coming along, very fast. It was the one Granny would be catching, she could tell by its number.

"Go on – now!" ordered Lorinda.

The boy pedalled furiously towards granny. The bus was slowing down just a little. It was twenty metres from the bus stop. Granny was looking towards it and putting her hand out to stop it. Now it was just short of the bus stop. The boy on the bicycle was nearly there. Then he shouted, and put on his brakes.

Granny turned round, leapt backwards across the pavement to safety, the boy skidded and slid right on to the road. Lorinda couldn't see the bus driver's face, but she could imagine the look of horror as he applied his brakes and the bus began to skid. There was a crunch.

Lorinda returned the fifty pence piece to her pocket and walked, rather shaken, back up the drive of the house.

A few minutes later her grandmother was back there as well.

"A stupid child!" she exclaimed. "He rode his bike along the pavement and straight into the path of a bus. Killed instantly, you know. It's quite shaken me up. I could have sworn he was aiming at me in the first place, the stupid boy. I'm going upstairs to lie down."

Lorinda went up to her room as well and stepped out on to the balcony. It stood directly over the front door, and the stonework being old was beginning to crumble here and there. She poked at one of the heavy stones experimentally. Definitely it was loose! She waggled it a bit more, and suddenly it came clean away. One push, and it would crash down on to the steps below.

This was highly dangerous. She thought she had better report it to Davies when he returned from his afternoon off so he could put it right. Then she had a better idea. She would report it to his wife immediately.

"There's a very loose stone on the balcony," she told the woman. "It's so loose that a strong wind, could blow it down."

"I'll tell Davies when he comes back," said Mrs Davies, "and he'll take a look at it.

Then Lorinda returned to the balcony and waited. She heard footsteps outside her room, and when she went to investigate, she found her grandmother going down the stairs in her outdoors clothes again. That meant she was going out. There was not much time!

She hurried out on to the balcony and waited. She heard the front door open and close. Then there was a pause. Granny would be putting her gloves on now, as she always did. Then she would step forward, and –

It was a clever idea to let Mrs Davies know about the loose stone beforehand because now it was certain to be thought an accident. She could not possibly be blamed when she had already reported the danger.

"One, and two, and three, and four, and five –" Lorinda knew how to count accurately in seconds, for she had read how in a book somewhere. You put an *and* in between the numbers and count slowly, and you were bound to be right ... "and eight, and nine, and ten, and *push*."

The stone fell, as expected, just as granny emerged from beneath the balcony where it overhung the steps. It thudded and splintered into pieces. Lorinda dashed out of her room without looking to see what had happened. She ran down the stairs two at a time, ready to report that she had heard the stone fall off.

She opened the front door, expecting to find her grandmother stretched out on the steps. Instead, granny was still standing, examining the pieces of broken stone curiously.

"I heard a crash," explained Lorinda.

"I should think you did! Go and tell Mason to come and pick up these pieces, will you? And don't go out on your balcony again until I've had the builders inspect it. It must be dangerous."

It was ridiculous that nothing was going right, Lorinda thought. In all the books she had read, people slipped on greased stairs, got pushed under buses, had great big stones fall on them, and invariably that was it – they were dead!

She went off to the greenhouse to water the plants, as she often did. It was nice and warm in there, away from stupid people, and very satisfying. She filled the watering can and started. There must be some other way which was absolutely certain to be effective. Then she would own everything, just as her parents had intended.

The old lemonade bottle was staring her in the face, with its top screwed on tight. A faded label, fastened on with sellotape, indicated that the bottle contained a herbicide. Herbicide? That was just another name for weedkiller!

The part-time gardener had made up some herbicide, but he had made too much. He had told Lorinda to leave the bottle alone because its contents were highly dangerous. In that bottle, he had said, was a sure poison with no antidote. Drink that and you'd be dead, he had said, hoping to frighten her. The bottle was still nearly half-full.

It was a pity that the label didn't state precisely which poison it was. She could have gone back into her father's study, looked it up in the dictionary and found out more about it. Or she could have read it up in the *Dictionary of Science*.

However ... granny went into the greenhouse sometimes. She could easily have drunk some herself, as far as anyone was likely to know. This was without doubt the answer to the problem! She should have thought of it before.

Her grandmother returned home in time for afternoon tea. When Lorinda was at home, her grandmother liked to take tea with her in the large drawing room overlooking the garden at the front of the house. Mrs Davies had laid everything out ready.

"I rather fancy coffee this afternoon, for a change," said her grandmother. "Would you go and ask Mrs Davies to bring a pot as well as this pot of tea? You'd prefer tea, I take it?"

Lorinda always preferred tea in the afternoon.

"That's all right, then," said her grandmother as Lorinda returned from the kitchen. She poured the tea for her granddaughter from a silver teapot and handed it to her.

"Cakes?"

Lorinda helped herself from the silver tray. She especially liked the big cream ones.

"Now," said her grandmother, settling back in her chair. "I think it's time we had a little chat. You'll be thirteen on your next birthday, won't you?"

Boarding school, that's what her grandmother was getting round to, Lorinda was certain of that. She was always on about how she ought to go away to a boarding school. Trying to get rid of her, that's what she was doing.

"Yes," she said, grimly.

32

"Now you know when your parents died – well, of course you do, you were there at the time, when they fell from that cliff – very distressing for you, I remember. Well they left all their money, this house and everything that goes with it to me."

Lorinda nodded.

"Don't gobble your food, Lorinda," said her grandmother, very kindly. "What perhaps you didn't know, since you were only eight at the time, was that it was all left to me only until you reached the age of eighteen. When you are eighteen it will all belong to you."

Mrs Davies entered with the coffee pot, and went out again. Granny tutted. She had forgotten her handkerchief.

"Oh, do drink your tea, Lorinda," she said impatiently. "I'll only be a moment."

This was the opportunity she had been waiting for. She had been wondering how to pour the weedkiller into granny's drink without her noticing, so as soon as granny had left the room she poured the entire contents of a little bottle which she had filled from the one in the greenhouse into the coffee pot. When granny returned, she was sipping her tea as if nothing had happened.

"Where was I? Oh yes. When you do inherit the estate I shall be left with nothing, absolutely nothing. You will look after me then, won't you?"

Lorinda scowled. She hadn't known that, but she was pretty sure that as soon as she was eighteen, granny would go – that was if she was still around then. Granny was watching her thoughtfully.

"No, I can see from your face that you will not. You will turn me out straight away, eh? Just as I thought."

She poured herself a coffee and began to drink it, not taking her eyes off Lorinda. "That would be a very cruel thing to do," continued granny very quietly.

Lorinda couldn't take her eyes off her grandmother now. She was waiting to see how quickly the weedkiller would begin to take effect. There was quite a lot in that coffee. Then granny was talking again.

"But another thing which perhaps you don't know is that should you not live to be eighteen, then all the money remains mine. That's how the will was written. So I've only got about five years to start planning for my retirement, haven't I? I don't think I can wait that long."

Lorinda poured herself another cup of tea, and drank it. The girl and her grandmother regarded each other in silence.

"So to save a lot of bother, I've been thinking. You often go into the greenhouse, don't you, to water the plants, so it's quite possible you could have drunk some of the contents from that old lemonade bottle in there. you know. You're stupid enough, I must say."

Lorinda nearly choked. Granny smiled.

"So I've put some weedkiller in the teapot," she concluded calmly, "and you've just drunk it. I can't wait another five years or so, you see, not knowing what you're going to do next all the time."

Then granny put her cup down on the table, trembling a little. Lorinda could tell by the expression on her face that she knew something was wrong.

As her grandmother collapsed, Lorinda hurried out into the kitchen, pushed past a surprised Mrs Davies and emptied the contents of a salt cellar into a cup, half-filled it with water and drank it rapidly. She had read somewhere that was how to make yourself sick. If she could be sick, she would be safe!

She was still trying to be sick as she died.

THE EMPTY TOMB

It was evening and, since they had nothing better to do, they were playing leapfrog over the gravestones. They were very old, so nobody tended them any more.

The more recent graves were down at the bottom of the slope where the land levelled out and a new wall had been built. They kept well away from them because several still had flowers on them and the grass was well trimmed by the relatives who would often visit on a Sunday.

But it wasn't Sunday, so nobody would mind very much, except the superintendent. He always told them to clear off, but he was off duty now. However, they still kept a wary eye open for him, just in case he should be passing by unexpectedly.

Fred thought he could jump a

gravestone which was taller than the others, but failed to open his legs wide enough. He crashed to the ground, laughing, and scrambled clear just as the stone itself wobbled and fell over.

"Nearly bloomin' flattened me, that one," chuckled Fred, looking at the fallen stone.

"Don't you think we ought to try and pick it up?" asked Simon, nervously. He looked around in case anyone had been watching.

John poked his fingers underneath, wriggled them a bit to get a better grip and tried to lift it. They all joined in, and between the three of them eventually managed to raise the stone upright into its hole.

But it fell down again.

"I think we ought to go," said Simon, "in case anyone comes."

"You're just scared," said Fred.

"He's always scared," scoffed John. "A real wuss, he is."

The other two looked at Simon contemptuously.

"No I'm not," Simon defended himself.

"Then, who was scared to walk through the woods by himself the other night when it was dark and spooky?" demanded Fred

"Well – because it was dark, I couldn't

see where the path was," said Simon.

"I went, didn't I, and by myself? You lost fifty pence, betting me that I wouldn't."

"John didn't go either," muttered Simon.

"Only because there wasn't any point in two of us going, one after the other, and I didn't bet him fifty pence. You were the one who did that," said John scornfully. "I didn't need to go."

"Well, go now then."

"All right. Any time."

They left the cemetery and set off towards the woods. It was only about half a mile before they reached them and, by the time they arrived, there was a wind blowing the trees about. While it wasn't very dark out in the open, among the trees, it was gloomy and definitely eerie.

"Going to bet me, then?" asked John.

Simon shook his head.

"No. You said you'd do it, so you just get on with it like you said."

"All right!" replied John stepping forward confidently into the woods. "How far do you want me to go?"

"As far as the fallen tree," said Simon firmly.

John disappeared along the narrow path, and they waited. About ten minutes later, he was back.

"Nothing to it," he said. "Now you."

"You'll wait for me, then?"

"We'll wait," promised John.

Simon went into the woods by himself. It was much darker now, especially in there. He paused to look back to where Fred and John were leaning against the first tree, watching his progress. Then he walked carefully deeper among the trees. The path meandered a bit and he found that if he concentrated on where he was putting his feet, it took his mind off what might be lying in wait for him on either side.

He was not scared of ghosts, he told himself. The woods were supposed to be haunted, but he'd never believed that. He was more scared of someone leaping out and attacking him than of the sight of a sudden spectre. They were not clawing hands trying to grab him as he walked past, but only twigs and branches catching on his clothes.

That rustling noise from somewhere on his left not far away must be a rabbit, or a bird moving about. Nothing to be afraid of at all. That was not a dark figure among the trees not more than a dozen paces away – though at first he thought it was – but only a bush stirring gently among the trees. It all smelt damp and mysterious, but that was all – just sounds and a damp smell.

He reached the fallen tree. It lay to the right of the path, almost alongside it. He stopped, counted to ten and turned to go back. There was nothing to it.

He was just in the very darkest part of the wood when he had the fright of his life. Without any warning, a terrific yell burst out from either side and two dark figures leapt on to the path in front of him. He jumped in terror. He just couldn't help himself.

"Scared you, then?" asked Fred, triumphantly.

"Er ... It was a bit of a surprise," admitted Simon, smiling wanly into the gloom. "But I wouldn't say I was scared. If I was, I would have turned round and run back!"

They considered the logic of that. It seemed to make sense.

"Let's go back to the cemetery and see if we can raise any spooks," suggested Fred.

"There aren't any such things as spooks," said Simon. "I reckon," he added, now it had been proved that he wasn't scared, "that what frightens people isn't spooks. It's just the dark, and not being able to see what's there. That's what scares some people."

They were back on the road again now, heading towards the cemetery and then home. John looked at Simon sideways.

"You reckon it's just the dark, then?" he said.

"Yeah. When you don't know what's out there."

"So you wouldn't mind spending the night in the cemetery, then?"

"Nothing to be scared of, is there?"

An idea was beginning to form in John's brain. He had it worked out in detail by the time they were back where they had started, by the fallen gravestone.

"I bet you daren't spend a night in one of those," he said, pointing to one of the eighteenth-century tombs which stood above the ground like stone boxes among the rest of the graves.

"There're bodies in there!" said Simon. "I wouldn't like to be in among dead bodies. It's not ... well ... it wouldn't be right."

"There aren't any bodies in there," said John, contemptuously. "Didn't you know that? These are just a bit of decoration on top. The bodies are underneath, buried like all the rest."

"How do you know?"

"I'll show you."

He led them to the nearest of the tombs.

"Now, you just grab hold of the top and push. Not too hard, we don't want it to fall off. Just heave at it."

He, Fred and Simon stood on one side of the tomb and began to push the lid. Nothing happened.

"All right, so that one's stuck. Let's try another."

They went to the next and tried again. This time the slab on top began to move slightly, and with much grunting and heaving they managed to slide the top across just a little way.

Then they peered inside. It was as John had said, quite empty inside. At the bottom they could make out bare earth and that was all.

"The bodies are underneath," repeated John, "like I said, but I still bet you daren't spend a night in one."

Simon examined what he could see of the inside.

"I'd suffocate," he said. "No air could get in."

"Of course you wouldn't. Enough air would get in there to last you for days."

"Well, all night would be silly. I'd get frozen stiff – and wet. It looks damp down there."

"Dry as a bone," said Fred, loftily. "Dry as a heap of bones, I should have said – get it?"

"Well, anyone could spend an hour in one of those," Simon said cautiously – "as long as he was sure somebody would turn up to let him out again."

"When it was pitch dark? I bet a fiver you wouldn't."

"You're on," said Simon.

"Tomorrow night, then. Nine o'clock,

when it's really dark. Then we'll come and let you out at ten."

Simon considered bleakly. He really had no choice now. He looked around. It must have been getting on for nine o'clock. Gloom was definitely settling in over the cemetery and the rest of the landscape. Very soon now it would be really dark.

"Okay," he decided, reluctantly, "but that one over there, by the wall. Just so you'll know exactly which tomb I'm in and won't spend half the night trying to find me."

They went over the wall and tried to shift the lid of the tomb he had pointed out. It stood by itself, so it couldn't be mistaken for any of the others. The lid moved surprisingly easily, and slid to one side as soon as they tried it. Furthermore, when they looked down into the empty space it was absolutely dry, almost comfortable-looking!

They were just sliding the lid back into place when a shout came from across the cemetery.

"You leave that alone!" came an angry voice – a woman's. "You just get out of here!"

They jumped over the wall, ran a little way and then looked back to see who it was. By this time, she was standing just the other side of the wall and shaking her fist at them.

"It's that Miss Hipcriss," said Fred.

"Who's Miss Hipcriss?"

"Oh, my uncle knows her. Says she's a

regular old nuisance. Always turning up at his farm at night asking for eggs. Old Crossy says the same, sometimes turning up at his shop just as he's closing, as if she couldn't be bothered to go shopping at the same time as everyone else. Lives in one of those terraced houses over there."

Simon couldn't remember ever having seen her before. She was a tall woman, slim and rather pale-looking, as far as he could tell in the fading light. But he'd certainly recognise her again from her large eyes.

"Go on, you boys, clear off!" she shouted at them.

"She collects stray cats as well," said Fred as they left slowly. "I don't know what she does with them. Sometimes she's got dozens. Then, next time you pass, there's just the odd one or two. Used to take in lodgers, too, but not any more. I'm not surprised. I expect her house reeks of cats."

"What does she feed them on?" John wanted to know.

Fred shrugged.

"Nobody knows. Old Crossy was telling someone the other day she never buys any cat food."

"Tomorrow night, then," said John abruptly to Simon.

"A fiver for one hour," said Simon firmly.

"Okay."

Promptly at nine o'clock, Simon was sitting on the wall outside the cemetery. He had with him a bar of chocolate, a piece of old sacking and a small pocket torch.

"What's the sacking for?" asked John.

"To sit on. Might as well be comfortable, mightn't I?"

They nipped over the wall, making sure that nobody was around to see them. They slid back the slab on top of the tomb. Simon slipped inside, spread out the sacking and sat on it. They closed the lid on him.

"Wait a minute!" they heard him shout from inside. They could hear him scraping his hands along the inside of the stone slab, and helped him open it wider.

"What?"

"Just seeing if I could get out by myself, in case you forgot to come back," Simon spluttered.

"We'll be back at ten," snorted Fred, "like we said."

And they slid the stone back into position again and left him.

This, thought Simon, was money for old rope. Any fool could sit in one of these things. How on earth did they think there was anything scary in this? It was dark all right – in fact it was pitch black inside there – but he could think of something much worse. Like being by yourself in the house at night.

He hated that.

If ever he was left alone at home and had to go upstairs, he always switched all the lights on first and then ran down the stairs afterwards. There was something about being left in a house by yourself at night, wondering whether in the dark somebody or something else might be there as well – especially if there was an odd creak on the staircase and no obvious explanation for it. But in here, why, it was almost cosy!

He took the torch from his pocket, switched it on briefly and flashed the light around. Not even a spider. He switched it off again, dug into his anorak pocket and pulled out his bar of chocolate. He dropped the wrapper on the ground. There was no point in being tidy because nobody would be poking around inside here for years.

He moved the sacking under his bottom slightly to make the seat more comfortable, settled back against the end wall of the tomb, and began to wonder who was buried beneath him. They must have been there a long time, whoever they were.

It was a strange feeling sitting there, knowing there was a rotting corpse only about a couple of metres away from him. Well, not rotting – it would certainly have rotted away by now, down to a skeleton.

He finished the chocolate. He ought to have brought a watch with him to keep track of the time. This was something he had completely forgotten. He wouldn't put it past them to leave him in the tomb for two hours. Since he had no watch, it would be very difficult to guess how long he'd been in there.

He wondered how it would feel to be a dead body lying in the tomb. He stretched out and lay flat, with his arms across his chest and just his head on the sacking. There was plenty of room at the end for his feet, so he wriggled down a bit further until his feet touched the other end wall.

There was a slight moment of panic as he worked his way back up to the other end. He seemed to be moving for ever before he reached the sacking. Then he found it, sat on it and leaned back.

He put his hand up and felt the slab above him. He could reach it easily. He put both hands up and gave a push. The slab didn't move, so he started pushing sideways with both hands flat against the underside of the stone, and felt it start to give.

If they were really intending to trick him, he couldn't see any great problem in getting out. If he had to, he could lie on his back and push hard with both feet, because his leg muscles were stronger than those in his arms and that would soon shift it.

It smelt a bit damp in there. It was almost like being in those woods the night before, but without any breeze. He drummed on the ground with his fingers. That was strange. It sounded hollow. He drummed again, then thumped with his fist.

That was very curious. He knelt up and patted the earth all along the floor of the tomb. It sounded hollow all the way along. On the other hand, perhaps it sounded like that because he was in a confined space. Out in the open, perhaps it would sound quite different. Unless, of course, below was really hollow!

Simon crawled about a bit more, not bothering to switch the torch on, for he knew where the edges were. Then, suddenly, near the far end of the tomb, he came across a small hole. He had just thumped again, and there it was – a hole big enough to put his fist into. He hadn't noticed it when he had shone a light round the tomb earlier.

He hoped the ground beneath him wasn't going to cave in and drop him down. Perhaps this hole was just a start. No, that was not at all likely. A snake's hole? No, too big. A rabbit's? Perhaps, but it wouldn't make much sense for a rabbit to come up inside here, because there would be no way out.

Buried treasure! Maybe somebody long ago had buried a box down there full of money and jewels and all that, and nobody was alive now who knew anything about it!

Since he was not likely to be bitten by

some animal, he might just as well put his hand down and see if he could feel anything of interest. He only hoped it wouldn't be a dead body just below the surface.

He put his hand down, reached a little further and suddenly, to his horror, a hand grasped his and held on!

In a real panic now, he switched on his torch in his other hand and saw that the whole of the far end of the ground was rising, but somehow the earth was not falling away from it. It was as if the soil had been stuck on to some sort of board, which was now folding over as if on a hinge.

Then he was free, struggling to open the roof of the tomb while somebody was sitting there in the tomb with him, watching him and smiling. She had a pale face and large eyes.

"Come closer," said Miss Hipcriss, climbing out very slowly ...

*   *   *   *   *

It was just after ten o'clock when Fred and John turned up at the cemetery. They jumped over the wall and began to swivel the stone slab to one side.

"Okay, you've won the bet," cried John – "if you're still in there, that is."

They opened the tomb and looked inside.

"Come on out, then," said Fred. "Hey,

you haven't suffocated, have you?"

Simon was lying on his back with his arms crossed over his chest. Fred felt worried about this, especially since his eyes were shut. Then he noticed the smile on his lips.

"Okay, stop playing about."

Simon stirred and his eyes opened, and he smiled broadly.

"Are you coming out or aren't you?" demanded John. "I've got your fiver in my pocket. What was it like in there, anyway?"

Simon slowly stood up and gazed at them thoughtfully. He looked rather pale, they thought.

"Are you sure you're all right?" asked John. "Hey, is that someone in there with you?"

"Come closer," said Simon. John did as he was asked and Simon sank his already enlarged fangs ever so gently into him.

Now Simon knew why Miss Hipcriss was never seen when the sun was out.

THE CREAK ON THE STAIRS

"We shan't be back until about two in the morning," said his mother. "So make sure you go to bed on time. No staying up to wait for us – right?"

Trevor nodded. He didn't really fancy the idea of being left all by himself, but there was something he wanted to try out and it would be best to try it when his parents weren't in. They might prevent him from doing it as they didn't hold with dabbling in that sort of thing.

They left for their party and Trevor was now alone. He went to bed reasonably early, because he wanted to get some sleep in first. He set his alarm clock for a quarter to midnight and went to sleep quickly.

It was Halloween, the night when devils are about and witches are supposed to go riding past. If you eat an apple and comb your hair at the same time as looking into a mirror at midnight on Halloween, then you will see a picture of the future appear in the mirror!

Another version, more for the girls, is that if you do the same at midnight on Midsummer's Day then you will see the one you will marry. But it was only the future that Trevor was interested in.

He heard the muffled buzzing from beneath his pillow where he had placed his alarm clock and woke at once. He put the clock back on the shelf by his bed. Just along the shelf he had left an apple and his comb and, lying face-down, the hand mirror from his parent's dressing table.

He felt along in the dark until he found them, then kept an eye on the luminous hands of the clock. Two minutes to go. That should be soon enough.

He sat up in bed, propped the mirror against his knees in front of him, picked up the comb in one hand and the apple in the other and took a small bite. Then he began to comb his hair. There was silence except for the ticking of the alarm clock, the gentle scratching sound from the comb across his head, and the munching of the apple.

Now that he was sitting up and his eyes were becoming more accustomed to the dark, the room became a little more distinct.

While the room was not actually growing lighter, the mirror definitely was. It was almost as if it was starting to brighten all by itself.

There was a movement in the glass, which Trevor knew must be the movement of his own reflection, but in the circumstances even that was rather eerie. He continued, half determined to see the thing through and half tingling with fear.

Then he looked closer into the mirror because there was certainly something odd happening. He was remaining perfectly still now, but something was moving in there as if someone was just behind him in the room.

He turned round sharply, but the only things behind him were the headboard of the bed and then the wall. Perhaps it really was going to work, then! Trevor felt quite excited at the prospect of actually seeing a picture of the future appear before him, like a film developing from an instant camera.

He felt rather than saw, that the mirror was beginning to glow by itself. Suddenly, like a shadow, a face appeared very faintly. Then it grew more distinct. Trevor munched and combed a little faster. It was a man's face – evil-looking. Trevor seemed to recognise him from somewhere.

He could now see more of this man. Not only was there a face, but two hands holding a rope between them as if coming towards him to strangle him. The smile on the man's face was more of a leer now. Something very unpleasant was going on in there!

The panic came when Trevor recognised who it was. He was the man who lived next door to them! He flung down the comb, dropped the apple core on the shelf and at once the picture faded to just an empty mirror with only a vague outline of his own reflection in it.

He turned the mirror over on to its face, trembling a little. What on earth could this mean? The man next door had only lived there for just a few months. He had hardly spoken to him. He lived by himself, and kept to himself. Nobody knew much about him. Perhaps that was it – a murderer living next door!

He heard a quiet creak on the stairs, and another, creeping up towards his bedroom. He searched for the handle of the mirror, found it, and grasped it firmly. It might just do for a weapon. Then there was no more sound. Just total silence. Here he was, in his bedroom with no way of escape except towards whoever was already on the stairs.

He held his breath and waited. His bedroom door was just slightly open because he had left it like that before he had gone to bed. Slowly, he turned his head and looked towards it, hoping against hope that it would not begin to open any further.

Very cautiously, so as not to make a sound, he began to draw his knees further up and to ease the bedclothes loose from where they had been tucked in at the side. Then, just as carefully, he slid his legs round until he was halfway out of the bed. He might stand a chance if, whoever it was, expected to find him lying helpless, instead of ready to make a dash past him.

However, there was no more sound, only the beating of his own heart, and that was beginning to steady down now. He was being silly, just frightening himself, he decided. That didn't explain the mirror, of course, unless he had been dreaming that. Perhaps he had fallen asleep halfway through the experiment. As for the creak on the stairs, that had been just a creak, like you get in many houses without explanation. If anyone had really been out there, he would have heard more than just two creaking sounds, he reckoned.

Keeping the mirror in his hand, just in case, he crept to the door. Almost crouching down, he gently nudged the door open a little wider and peered out. It was dark, so he could see nothing, but what he was actually doing was proving to himself beyond all doubt that he could hear nothing out there either.

He listened very carefully, first for the

sound of breathing, and then for any sounds from downstairs. He realised that if there were any burglars downstairs he would have heard them breaking in, because both the front and back doors were locked and all the downstairs windows shut tight. They would have had to have broken a pane of glass to get in and that would have woken him up.

So, feeling brave, he switched on his bedroom light and straightened his bed, casting an occasional glance at the bedroom door just in case it should start to open. There had not been another sound from out there since those two creaks.

"Is that you – Mum, Dad?" he called. He expected no answer, of course, but needed to hear the sound of his own voice to ensure that everything was back to normal.

There was no answer, so he was still entirely by himself. He even plucked up courage to step out on to the landing and look down the stairs. There was just enough light from his bedroom to be able to see quite clearly that the staircase was deserted.

Then he thought of the apple core which he had left on the shelf and decided to take it downstairs to the bin to avoid awkward questions in the morning. He switched the landing light on, went back into his room, picked up the remains of the apple and was about to return to the landing when he heard it again.

There was another creak on the stairs! He hesitated, but since the light was on, he walked out on to the landing. It was not half as scary with the two lights on, the one in his bedroom and the one on the landing.

Nothing. Just as he had thought. He was halfway down, when the front door rattled. Although the landing light was on behind him, the hall light was not and down there it was very dim.

Then he heard the sound of a faint breeze blowing outside which explained the rattle. The wind must have caught it, that was all. He continued down the stairs. There was another rattle, but it didn't sound like the wind this time.

The door was secure and nothing could get in unless he opened it. So he gently prised at the letter-box flap with his finger nails until it lifted, then put his eyes close and looked out.

A dark figure was standing there, motionless – not directly outside the front door but just a little distance away. It was dark, so he couldn't make him out distinctly, but he was out there all right. Trevor dropped the flap quickly, and wondered what he should do.

It was then that he sensed something behind him – not directly behind him, but a little distance away up the stairs. He turned at once. Half-way down the stairs was a shadow which should not have been there. It was like a man in dark clothes looking down at him.

The stairs creaked yet again, and the shadow began to move upwards. There was another creak, this time from the landing itself. The figure was *going into his room*!

It was at this point that Trevor really began to panic! He could not go out of the front door, because of the figure lying in wait for him out there. That dark, motionless figure through the letter-box had not been his imagination, he was certain of that. He could not return upstairs because there was something up there, too! He was trapped!

On a little table just inside the front door was the telephone. At least he still had some contact with the outside world. He picked it up. He was not sure who to call, but if he couldn't think of anyone else, he would dial the police.

At least somebody might come and help him – or perhaps prevent him from being ... well, he was not sure what.

A shadow on the stairs could hardly strangle him, but whoever was outside just might find some way to get in.

The telephone was dead. There was not even a crackle from it. He couldn't ring anybody. Something must have gone wrong with the line. Had somebody outside cut the wires so he couldn't telephone? That was ridiculous! Nobody would have any reason to do that ... unless it was a maniac.

No, it was the darkness, that was scaring him. It was time he pulled himself together. All this and the telephone being out of order as well, it must be a coincidence.

He raised the letter-box flap again. Just as he thought – there was nobody out there at all. Either that man hadn't been there and he'd imagined him, or he had been there but had now gone away. And the shadow on the stairs – well, that had just been a shadow.

He walked into the kitchen to drop the apple core into the bin, switching on the light first as soon as he was within reach of the switch. He went into the living room where he also turned on the light. Half the house was lit up now, but he didn't care. As he made his way back upstairs he would make sure he turned them off behind him.

If felt safe in the living room, where everything was well lit and familiar. He glanced at the clock on the wall: nearly twenty-past twelve. The seconds hand was moving round steadily in a very comforting way. Everything was back to normal.

Unfortunately, he heard yet another creak on the stairs, followed by another and another. This time it sounded just as if somebody was coming downstairs, for the last creak was lower down, and not so loud, as if somebody was trying to be very quiet.

The creaks stopped. He ran swiftly towards the windows. If he had to, he would open one of them and climb out and run for help. He drew the edge of the curtain back and gasped in horror. Just outside the house he saw that dark figure again, looking directly towards the house! He dropped the curtain quickly, his heart pounding.

There was just one chance. If he could get to the back door, open it, run out into the garden, he could escape that way. He must remember not to climb over the fence of the house where the man next door lived.

Taking a deep breath, he flung the living room door open wide and dashed quickly through the kitchen to the back door. He unbolted it as quickly and as quietly as he could, glancing behind him rapidly from time to time as he loosened the bolt. As he turned the key and partly opened the door he heard the creak on the stairs again.

Somehow, from where he was, the sound was different.

It did not now seem to be in his house at all. Opening the back door a little wider in case he had to bolt through it, he walked steadily towards the door of the kitchen leading into the hallway and listened again, more carefully this time.

Yes, there was still creaking! Yes, it was on the stairs, but it was now clear that it was not coming from their stairs, but from the stairs of the house next door.

He went boldly into the hall now and put his ear to the adjoining wall. Without a doubt, it was the man next door, climbing the stairs. That was what had been frightening him all along. He realised now – apart, of course, from the face in the mirror. He was not quite convinced that he had not seen that, but the creaking on the landing must have been next door's landing.

However, had he really imagined the shadow on the stairs? It had seemed real enough at the time, but then, in the dark, and in a panic, one could imagine anything.

He heard a whistling from somewhere outside the front door as he took his ear from the wall. He ran into the living room, turned the light off, and drew back the edge of the curtain, so that he could see out without being seen. The figure out there was moving away now with what looked like a dog following him. So that explained it. Nothing to be frightened of anywhere.

Trevor went into the kitchen. It was a fine night outside. He had never been out in the back garden in his pyjamas before. It didn't feel all that cold, so he stepped outside to take a look at the stars before going back to bed. He didn't feel at all sleepy now.

There was only one tree of any size growing in any of the gardens along his road, and that was their apple tree. Trevor decided to run to the tree and back, just to prove to himself that there really was nothing to be afraid of. Then he would lock up and go back to bed again, and forget the whole silly nonsense about the mirror, the creaking and everything else.

He had almost reached the tree when he realised there was somebody there, just in front of him! He stopped dead, petrified. That somebody seemed too tall, almost as if suspended in space beneath the thickest branch.

It was the eyes staring at him which really startled him. Whoever it was didn't move. Then, the light from the open kitchen door, revealed the man from next door, hanging from the tree with a rope round his neck.

Trevor stepped forward and gently touched his hand. It was stone cold. He must have been hanging there for hours.

DEADLY CREATURE

At the inquest, the coroner regarded the boy solemnly over the top of his half-moon glasses. This boy certainly did not seem to be strong enough, or vicious enough, to have committed murder. But something was certainly wrong.

"Do you mean to tell me," the coroner said, "that you had no part at all in these horrible deaths?"

"It wasn't my fault," said the boy.

"That wasn't what I asked," said the coroner, calmly. "Did you have any part in killing them, or in killing an unfortunate school-fellow of yours?"

"No. Nothing at all," said the boy.

"But you do know something of how they died?"

"Oh, I know all right," said the boy.

*   *   *   *   *

It was horrible! Ian had first noticed it only a few moments before and thought it was just the wind blowing things about. Now he was sure it had to be something quite different.

First the tall grasses at the very edge of the field began to rustle, apparently for no reason, but Ian took no notice. Then it happened again, only this time much nearer to him. Then the hedge began to sway right alongside him, and a hole appeared in it.

As he walked along, hurrying now, more holes appeared. They seemed to be following him. Then the holes stopped appearing and only the grass at the edge of the field was moving aside, or being crushed, as if a huge animal was treading on it.

Ian began to run. He reached the gate at the end of the field, scrambled over it and paused to look behind him to see if he had shaken the thing off. There was no more movement in the field, but now all round him, the ground was being pressed down as if he were being circled by some enormous creature.

There were no definite footprints, just – movement! Whatever was causing it seemed to have jumped over the gate, as if following him. He felt that whatever it was wanted to tear him as it had torn large holes in the sturdy hawthorn hedge.

But nothing more frightening than that happened. When Ian moved, it moved. It was like being followed by a playful dog, but one which he could not see and which was of a tremendous size.

Now what would he have done if it had been one of those? He would simply point back the way he had come, and say something like, "Go away! Go on, go back home!"

He tried it. All that happened, was that a flattened patch was made on the ground, as if the thing was sitting there and watching him.

"You wait 'til I spread this round the school," said a voice behind him.

Ian turned round, startled at being found doing such a ridiculous thing as talking to thin air.

"Do you talk to the trees and clouds as well?" asked the other boy. "How about the curtains at home?"

"Shut up," replied Ian, fiercely. "Don't you go telling anybody."

However, Ian knew it was too late. Chris Higgins would delight in spreading any rumour which would make him look stupid. He was like that. They had disliked each other ever since infants school and, as they got older, Ian had always tried to avoid him, but Chris was always there, goading him, trying to make him look small or stupid in front of everyone else.

"You wait 'til I tell everybody about this," chuckled Chris. "I'm going to make you look the right idiot you are, talking to imaginary animals."

"Shut up," hissed Ian. "If you breathe a word ... I'd explain, except you wouldn't understand."

"So you're saying I'm thick now, are you?" said Chris, getting ready for a fight.

He was spoiling for a fight, knowing that it would end up as always with Ian getting the worst of it. Ian was sick of it, but with nobody else around he knew he wasn't going to escape easily. Chris usually managed to pick a fight when there were no witnesses.

"Get out of my way," said Ian.

Chris was taking his coat off.

"Better start running," he said, "while you've still got the chance."

"You know you can beat me," complained Ian, "and you can run faster than me, so why don't you leave me alone?"

"Because I like beating you up, that's why. Go on, then – run, like you always do. 'Til I catch you."

There was that movement again, just a few paces away, but only Ian seemed to have noticed it.

"I'm not running," said Ian. "I think perhaps I should warn you ... "

The first blow caught Chris on the side of his head. He stumbled, tripped over the uneven ground and shielded his head from the next blow which he knew was coming.

The second blow never arrived. Instead, Chris gave a kind of gurgling scream, and when Ian looked up he seemed to be struggling with something. He was on his back, fighting the air with his fists and kicking. Then he tried to get up and run, but the next second he was flat on the ground with blood pumping out of him. Then he lay still.

Ian cautiously approached Chris. Chris was still gurgling. Then it stopped. At first Ian was surprised and then curious. He had never seen anyone with his throat torn open before. Then he ran like the wind and didn't stop until he was in the street, amongst other people.

There was no sense in telling anybody. For one thing, what he had just seen couldn't be explained to anyone. In any case, it was too late now to do anything for poor Chris because he was certainly dead. He was shaking as he walked along the street to his home, but tried to hide it.

Oddly, he found that the horrific sight had not made him feel sick, or even ill. Fear overcame all of that, including what might yet happen to himself, but somehow it seemed that whatever force had caused that terrific injury had done it to protect him. Like an alsatian or a rottweiler might leap on whoever attacked its master.

It was frightening, though, to have a force like that protecting him. He hadn't ordered it. It had just happened. That made it worse.

"Where have you been?" his mother asked him when he got home.

"Just walking about," he said.

"You've been over those fields again," said his mother. "I can tell from the state of your shoes. Now you go out the back and scrape that mud off before you have your tea. Go on!"

His father stopped reading the paper.

"Get those filthy shoes off the new carpet!" he shouted angrily, getting up. "Go on, do as your mother says, or – "

Ian saw the carpet near his father's chair depress slightly. Then the chair itself moved just a fraction as if something had brushed heavily against it.

"Dad!" warned Ian in alarm. "Stay still!"

His father was in no mood to be argued with. Perhaps his day had not gone well for him so far, or maybe the news in the paper was depressing. He flung the paper down into the chair and moved toward his son.

70

Ian looked round the room in a panic. He tried to guess where the creature was and flung himself to stand in front of his father. At once, two holes appeared in the new carpet, side by side but nearly a metre apart, as if claws had torn into it as a fierce animal had pulled up suddenly before leaping.

"What the hell!" exclaimed his father in astonishment, looking down at the damage. "Judy, come and look at this! It just – well, it just happened. There must be some nails sticking up from the floorboards."

While his parents pondered over the holes in the carpet, Ian dashed out to the back of the house, took off his shoes and began to scrape the mud from them. He didn't want to be the one who had to explain.

One thing was now absolutely certain. Whatever this thing was, it was inside the house. What seemed almost as sure was that it had somehow taken a fancy to him and if anyone was going to be harmed, it would not be him.

He kept a wary eye open all through that evening, trying to track down where the creature might be. As he watched the television, sitting on the sofa, he felt it move slightly as if something was leaning against it.

His mother, at the other end of the sofa, regarded him quickly for a moment as if she felt it as well. He knew she was glancing in his direction, so he kept his eyes firmly on the screen. He knew she didn't like him wriggling about on the furniture, so he made sure she could see that he was sitting still.

When he went to bed, he knew that the creature had gone upstairs and was now inside the room with him. He could imagine it lying down on his rug as he turned the light out. He did try feeling about with his hand in the dark, trying to find it, but with no result. Whatever it was, he could neither see it nor feel it. But it was *there*, he knew that beyond all doubt, and he also knew that it could see him.

The finding of Chris's body caused a tremendous uproar. *"Senseless killing"* screamed the newspapers, and the reports went on for days. Several children from the school went to his funeral, but Ian was not one of those who were chosen.

Then came the first reports of dogs and cats found dead and half-eaten. That caused even more alarm. Some savage killer was on the loose and likely to attack both animals and humans. At first, it was believed to be a gorilla which had escaped from the nearby safari park, but this turned out not to be true. When the keepers pointed out that, even if one ever did escape, it was unlikely to eat dogs and cats, people became convinced that it was the work of a human lunatic.

Until this man was found, parents

were warned that children should be escorted to and from school each day and elderly people were advised to remain indoors, or only venture out in pairs. Everyone was warned to keep alert at all times and to make sure that their pets were fastened up securely.

What Ian did notice was that, shortly before the latest report of a dead animal came out, he saw no evidence of the creature around him for an hour or so. Then, sooner or later it would be back, just as if it had returned home. He could imagine it curling up sleepily on the hearth-rug, or lying in his bedroom.

It never went into school with him, either. He knew it was there as he walked to school (with a group nowadays because the parents insisted). He felt it running alongside if they were taken in a parent's car. Also, he knew it was waiting for him each afternoon when he came out. Like a faithful dog protecting him all the time, he thought.

Slowly the panic died down and people began to relax again. The verdict for the death of Chris had been murder "by a person or persons unknown". Still various animals were found dead and partly-eaten from time to time, but now the reports tended to come from farther away. Now Ian noticed that the creature was absent for slightly longer than before. He knew why. It had to travel further to catch its prey.

At least, he assumed this creature was responsible. He couldn't think of any other explanation. Not that he blamed it in the slightest. After all, it had to eat, just like anything else. He decided on a little test to find out if he was right.

Against the back wall of his house stood a rabbit hutch. In it was his bad-tempered rabbit, Whitey. It had never been a pet. Right from the start, if anyone put a hand inside its hutch, the rabbit would make a growling noise and try to bite it. Consequently, it was hardly ever let out because of the difficulty of catching it afterwards.

One afternoon, when he had returned home from school, Ian opened the rabbit's hutch door and enticed it out on to the lawn. He knew the creature was nearby because of the unmistakable signs. He also knew that the creature would never touch anything it thought belonged to Ian, like it had made no further attack on his father.

His father was Ian's property, the creature seemed to think, like his mother, or his rabbit, or any of his friends, so they were perfectly safe. This time, though, Ian walked right up to Whitey with his hand held out. At once the rabbit growled, ready to bite or scratch, as it always did.

Ian drew back, then pointed at the rabbit, looking round to where he knew the creature to be.

"Get him!" he said loudly.

Whitey was torn into two pieces at once, and one half disappeared. The front half lay still for a moment, then was shaken about and then that went, too. The rabbit was simply no longer there, apart from one mangled paw.

"Good God!" Ian heard his father say.

He turned at once. His father was looking at him curiously, as if afraid of him. He came on to the lawn and inspected the paw from a safe distance.

"Ian. What have you done?" whispered his father.

Ian decided to tell the truth.

"Now you know about Chris, and about those missing dogs and cats, don't you?" he said calmly. It was a sufficient explanation.

"I don't understand," said his father, weakly. "What power have you got to make a thing like that happen?"

Ian could tell the way his father's mind was working. He was thinking that it was Ian himself who had the power, and was suddenly afraid.

"It's not me, it's the creature. You're quite safe. So is Mum, and any of our friends. It doesn't mean any harm. It's just that it's got to eat, and Chris – well, he started to fight me. The creature protects me. Look – you can even tell where he is."

His father looked around him in bewilderment. So Ian went over to where the creature was and it soon became clear what he meant. The movements began on the grass and among the flower beds at the side.

"He's with me most of the time," said Ian truthfully.

After some discussion that night, Ian's mother suggested that she should let her brother, Ian's uncle, come and talk to him about this. He was a biologist at the university and would be very interested. Since he was one of the family, the matter could be kept quiet for the time being.

Ian didn't have any objection, so his uncle, rather sceptically, turned up the following evening. They sat in the living room, side by side on the sofa.

"Where is he now, then?" asked his uncle. This, he was thinking, was a case for a psychiatrist.

"Right next to me," said Ian.

"You mean you can see him, then?" asked his uncle, humouring him.

"No."

"Then how do you know he's there?"

"You can tell by the signs."

"What signs?" Clearly his nephew was making this up as he went along.

"Watch the carpet," said Ian, getting up and walking across the room. Then he looked towards the end of the sofa where he had just been sitting and patted the hearth rug. "Come on, boy," said Ian.

His uncle felt the sofa move as if something huge had brushed against it. Then, he saw the pile of the new carpet depress as invisible paws padded over it. Ian returned to the sofa.

"Do you believe it now?" he asked. "You could always pretend to attack me, of course, but if you did you'd end up with your throat torn out. He just wouldn't understand the difference between pretend and real, you see."

Ian didn't really care what his uncle thought because he didn't like him much anyway. He doubted that his mother did either, even though he was her brother. He was too pompous, too sure of himself, too superior to anyone he thought less clever than himself.

His uncle was, however, extremely impressed, and also very excited. He tried to hide his excitement.

"So, you have a creature, totally unknown to science, which is unseen and unheard," he said, slowly. "We can't touch it, but clearly it can both see and hear us, and contact us if it wants to."

"I've never actually felt it," Ian had to admit.

"No, but I bet your rabbit did – and

those others. Perhaps it's something to do with the speed at which it moves," said his uncle thoughtfully. "I think I know something about it already."

Then he fell silent, regarding the hearth rug as if trying to make out the outline of the creature he was now convinced was lying there.

"What do you know already?" Ian was curious.

"Human ears can only hear within certain limits. That's why dogs can hear dog whistles but we can't. Something similar with bats. Now –" His uncle became even more thoughtful.

"Go on," said Ian, impatiently.

"What I was going to say is that whatever sounds this creature makes must be beyond our human range. That's why we can't hear it growl, for example. It growls either too high or too low for us to hear."

Ian couldn't imagine that the creature would have a high-pitched growl. It didn't seem to fit somehow.

"And our sight is very limited as well. Most people don't realise that. We can't see anything beyond the infra-red and ultra-violet ends of the spectrum. In fact, we can't even see ultra-violet or infra-red light at all, but only their effect. Isn't that so?"

Ian was not quite sure he understood all that, but he readily agreed.

"So this creature, whatever it is, makes noises outside our range of hearing, and has a colour so far on one side or the other of our spectrum that we can't see it. So, it's totally silent and totally invisible. Yes! That must be the explanation! Wait here a moment."

He strode out of the room. Ian could imagine the creature looking up to make sure his uncle was not about to attack him, then settling down again when it was satisfied. His uncle returned from where he had parked his car with a large black case in one hand and, in the other, a lamp-like arrangement with an electric cord and plug hanging from it.

He opened the case, took out another electric lead and plugged both of them into the power-point for the television. He set the lamp on a small table, pointed it towards the hearth rug, and switched it on. At once a pulsating beam of light came from it. He adjusted the speed of the pulses with a control knob.

"Tell me if you see anything," he said excitedly.

Ian watched the hearth rug.

"What is that?" he asked.

"A stroboscope," replied his uncle. He left the lamp pulsating while he switched off the room light. "There's just a chance it might produce results," he added as he kept adjusting the speed of the flickering light.

Just for a moment, Ian thought he could see something looking at him. It was only for a second or so, but what he saw looked rather like an enormous wolf. It was very hairy and had, what seemed to be, long claws, tucked up for the moment like a cat's claws. It occupied the whole of the hearth rug, and seemed so wide that he was surprised it could get through the door.

Ian described it as accurately as he could, from the brief time he had been able to see it.

"It was only a sort of outline, though," he explained. "I couldn't see what colour it was."

His uncle nodded with satisfaction.

"Just as I thought," he said. He switched the stroboscope off and put the living room light back on. Then he opened the lid of the black case and inside was a row of dials and knobs.

"Now for its hearing," he said, and switched on.

When he held a pair of earphones towards the hearth rug, Ian could hear coming from them, quite loudly, a high-pitched note. As the knobs were adjusted, the pitch went higher and higher, and finally disappeared altogether as the note passed beyond the range of human hearing.

"He's going out," said Ian in surprise,

seeing the signs that the creature was moving towards the door. Then the door itself moved.

His uncle switched off his equipment and grinned all over his face.

"Exactly as I thought," he said, beginning to pack his equipment away. Then he added, "I'd like to capture this creature. It would make the biggest stir ever if I could. We'd become world famous," he said, beaming.

Ian knew exactly what his uncle had in mind.

He didn't want his creature captured, experimented on and investigated.

"No!" he shouted angrily.

His parents, who had remained in the other room while his uncle conducted his experiments, came running in.

"He wants to trap it," Ian shouted, "and he's not going to!"

He made sure that he didn't point at his uncle or make any threatening move, for he knew what would happen if he did. Now the sounds had been switched off, he had noticed the door shudder again – just once.

"It's all right," said his mother, soothingly. "Nobody's going to do anything you don't want. And now it's time for bed. Up you go."

"Goodnight," said Ian curtly to his uncle, and obediently went upstairs.

He could hear them talking when he was in his room, but not quite loud enough to make out what they were saying. He did hope his parents were dissuading his uncle from trying to do anything foolish.

It was a week later. Ian had been in bed for quite a while, but was not asleep. He could hear the sound outside his bedroom door of people talking very quietly and then something being dragged away.

It was strange for visitors to come so late. He wondered if the creature, in the bedroom with him, was being kept awake as well, but of course he had no way of knowing.

Then he heard his father calling to him, quietly.

"Ian, I want you out here, quickly."

So he got out of bed, opened his bedroom door and went out on to the landing, still sleepy. Immediately, his father grabbed him and pulled him away from the door. Then his uncle and three men he'd never seen before slammed the door shut behind him and began to slide against it what looked like a big steel box. It was on rollers and seemed to be very strong and heavy.

He was wide awake at once.

"No, you mustn't!" he cried. "You don't know what you're doing!"

But he knew very well what his stupid uncle and his friends were trying to do. He could guess they had come from the university. They knew that when he went to bed the creature always went up with him. So now they had enticed him out and the creature was left behind.

The solid steel cage fitted the doorway exactly. Two of the men were on top, holding a steel shutter between them which fitted into a slot at the end of the cage nearest his bedroom. As soon as the creature came out, they would slam the shutter down and trap it inside.

Everybody had tricked him. He didn't blame his parents, who no doubt had been persuaded that this was for the best, but he certainly did blame his uncle and his uncle's friends.

There was first an urgent scratching in the bedroom.

"The university will pay for the damage to the door, of course," his uncle was saying, excitedly. "That's all arranged. No problem. And it's all in the interests of science, as I told you."

The scratching stopped. There was a sudden splintering crash as the creature leaped clean through the wood of Ian's bedroom door. As soon as that happened the two men on top of the steel box dropped the shutter down. The box rocked slightly as the creature landed inside it.

"We don't know its weight, of

course," his uncle was saying, "but I don't imagine it to be exceptionally heavy, just strong. We should have very little problem in sliding the reinforced box down the stairs and on to the lorry."

"You don't know how strong, do you?" yelled Ian. "You just don't know. And by the time you find out, it'll be too late. Mum, Dad – get downstairs – quick!"

The box was beginning to rock about now, so they needed no more urging and fled. Ian stood his ground.

"Open the front door," he shouted down the stairs.

He was safe – he knew that. The creature would not think he had anything to do with this. But he didn't give much for the chances of his uncle and his uncle's friends. However, he still tried to help. If they would just all go downstairs, he would let the creature out and everyone would be safe.

"You just stand clear so the rollers don't run over your feet," instructed his uncle. Obviously he was going to take no notice of Ian's warning. "Then as soon ... "

That was as far as he managed to get before the end of the reinforced steel box burst open like an explosion! The steel bent outwards to form a large hole as if it had been torn like tissue paper. Two more holes appeared in the carpet on the landing as the creature leapt out.

It turned so quickly that Ian could feel the air move past him. The four men lay dead. His uncle's head rolled away from his body a few inches before it stopped. Ian was horrified, but couldn't have done anything to prevent it.

The stair carpet showed a series of depressions and a faint trail of blood. The creature was gone from the house!

*　　*　　*　　*　　*

The coroner's voice sounded rather tired and his face was set unpleasantly as he looked across again at Ian.

"So, Ian, if you are saying that what we have just heard is the truth, then I had better remind you ... "

"It's the truth, all right," interrupted Ian. "You see, if something's beyond our range of vision because its colour is too far beyond one end or other of the spectrum ... "

"Yes, yes," snapped the coroner, testily. "We've all heard what you say was your late uncle's theory. But can you honestly expect us to believe ... "

"I think there might be more than this one creature," interrupted Ian. "I don't see why not."

The coroner moved irritably in his chair.

"Now look here, my boy, we've heard the evidence from the police, and from the surgeon who conducted the post-mortem on all of these victims."

He was pointing at Ian wagging his finger at him angrily. Ian interrupted again, very quietly.

"Please, sir, I wish you wouldn't make threatening movements like that. It's not safe, you know."

"Why isn't it safe?"

"I just don't think you'd better, that's all."

The coroner abruptly laid his hand on his lap as he stared towards where Ian was now looking. In the hard wooden floor of the courtroom, barely a few paces from where Ian stood, a series of splintered holes had begun to appear as if huge claws had just been dug into the wood.

"I really don't think you should ..." said Ian.

THE BODY CHANGER

He was only half-awake when he felt the cold hand touching his face. It must have been the coldness of the hand which had woken him in the first place. Then, as soon as he began to stir, it stopped. Dan opened his eyes cautiously.

Of course he wouldn't be able to see anything and it had probably only been a dream anyway. Perhaps it was like that horrible time when he had woken up to find his left arm dead, completely useless. That had really frightened him until he realised that he had been lying so awkwardly on it, he had somehow managed to cut off the circulation. It was perfectly all right again after a minute or so.

Or maybe it was like that other time, when he was convinced he was being strangled and could feel the hand round his throat. He had really panicked then, until he realised it was his own hand, which during the night had somehow got tucked under his chin.

But this was different. To his horror, he could see a wispy figure standing at the side of his bed. Then it faded very slowly and finally disappeared.

The next night exactly the same thing happened – the cold hand, the waking up, the figure by his bed. Only this time he heard the figure speak, quite distinctly, but as if a long way off.

"I am going to take your body," it said. It was an oldish man, not very tall and with a wrinkled face as far as he could tell.

Dan was almost convinced he was still dreaming and shut his eyes again until he was properly awake. But when he opened them a second time, the figure was still there.

"I need your body," said the figure. This time he seemed to draw back the bedclothes just a little, find Dan's hands and took hold of them. They felt icy cold as the figure bent over the bed and stared into Dan's eyes.

He could feel himself fading away, slipping into nothingness. It was as if he was being drawn out of his body, or as if this old man was melting into his. Now the figure drifted on to the bed, still holding his hands firmly.

"Don't resist and it will be easy," the man was saying.

Dan managed to stir himself, shake the hands off, leap out of bed and switch the light on. The figure was still on the bed, almost there, almost not.

"I shall have you," it said, before fading away again.

Dan was scared to go back to bed now. The figure might have vanished, but there was no knowing if it wasn't still somewhere in the room with him. He looked around to draw comfort from the familiar surroundings, then felt round the bedclothes to find if he could feel anything of this strange visitation.

The bed seemed to be all right now. He got back in and lay down. He waited. Whatever it had been had definitely gone now. He climbed out, turned the light off and felt his way back into the bed. He slept soundly for the rest of the night.

On his way to school the next morning, Dan saw the figure again. Dan was waiting at the bus stop, when the white-haired man just in front of him turned round and looked straight at him. It was the same man, except he was not a wispy figure drifting in space now, but a real human being.

He was in his seventies, wearing an

old overcoat which hung open to reveal a brown suit underneath and old brown shoes, brightly polished. The old man smiled, not a friendly smile, but one which seemed to hint at some kind of secret between them.

"Good morning," he said, slowly. Then he nodded once or twice before turning his back on Dan again.

Dan let the bus leave without him. He was sure he must have imagined the same old man who had appeared in his bedroom on the previous two nights. Yet he was almost certain now that he had seen him somewhere else – outside the school gates, or walking along the road at home-time.

Dan walked to school that morning because it was as quick as waiting for the next bus. He would still just about get there on time.

"Dan, get on with your work!" snapped the maths teacher. "Stop day-dreaming."

Dan hardly heard him, for he was staring at the window on the corridor side of the classroom. Looking in at him was the same old man!

"I ... I think somebody in the corridor wants you, sir," he stammered.

The maths teacher opened the classroom door and looked up and down the corridor.

"You're imagining things," he said.

"There's nobody there at all. Get on with your work."

Later, when they were on their way to their next lesson, the old man was leaning against a wall in the corridor. But perhaps it was only his imagination because nobody else seemed to notice he was there.

"Isn't this corridor cold?" commented Dan's friend Craig as they passed where the old man was standing. "Just as you turn the corner, I mean. That's funny, it's warmed up again now."

Craig wandered back to test it, passing the old man and then coming back to join them. It was obvious that he still hadn't seen the figure.

"It's just that one place, like somebody's left a refrigerator door open."

"Must be a window open somewhere," said someone else.

Only Dan knew the real reason! He remembered hearing that whenever a ghost was supposed to appear, it often felt colder. Others were coming along the corridor behind them now, and still the old man stood, ignoring them and watching only Dan. When Dan turned to look back just before going into the classroom, the figure had vanished.

On the way home, he saw him again. This time he was just as solid as when he had met him at the bus stop that morning. He must really have been there now because some girls walking along the pavement separated to let him pass.

None of this made sense. If he was a ghost, then he wasn't really there. But if he was real, why could nobody else see him in the school corridor? Dan had a horrible feeling he was going mad. There was no way anyone could be both real and imaginary at the same time – or was there?

Before closing his bedroom curtains that night, Dan looked carefully up and down the street. There was nobody in sight, but next moment, there in front of him was the smiling, wrinkled face of the old man!

He yanked the curtains shut and felt himself sweating with fear. This was absolutely impossible – the man was floating in the air outside his bedroom window! He took a long time to undress and climb into bed that night, fearing that the figure would appear beside him and perhaps even speak to him again. It took even longer before he finally fell asleep.

The cold touch of a hand woke him again. He sat up with a start to find that the figure seemed to be glowing faintly in the darkness.

"You can't escape, you know," the man said, slowly. It was very strange. He was standing right next to him, yet the voice seemed to come from further away, like the sound coming from a television in the distance.

"Why are you here?" demanded Dan, very quietly. He didn't want to wake anyone else in the house.

"I told you, I want your body."

"I'm going nuts," said Dan. "You're not there at all."

When the figure tried to take hold of his hands again, Dan quickly hid them under the bedclothes. At once the figure faded away. Dan lay down again.

He thought he lay down, but the whole thing was so crazy that he couldn't be certain he had ever really woken up. More than likely he had dreamt the whole thing, was still dreaming and had never woken up at all! He'd had dreams like that before, but then he had always known they were dreams and had been able to shake himself out of them.

He *must* have been dreaming this time because suddenly the man was there again. He was saying:

"Wake up, so that I can take your body."

"Why must I be awake, then?" Dan found himself asking.

"Because you must be awake for me to take you over."

He woke at once, though now he was struggling not to. The figure was there now, coming closer.

"Give me your hands," he was saying, trying to take hold of them.

Dan remembered how he had felt himself fading away like a ghost when this creature had managed to grasp his hands. So he sat on them firmly.

"I shall be back," hissed the old man, and disappeared.

His mother noticed how tired Dan looked the following morning.

"I didn't sleep very well," he explained.

"It seems to me that you've not been sleeping very well for the last few nights," said his mother. "Been having some bad dreams?"

"No, no," he said, shrugging it off. After all, how could he possibly explain what was really going on? If he did, he'd be taken straight off to the doctor! And there was nothing wrong with him, except there must be something odd inside his mind at the moment. Better to leave it and let it put itself right. It was bound to turn out properly in the end – or so he hoped.

"You're going to bed early tonight, anyway," his mother decided. "You need to catch up on all that sleep you've been missing."

It was football that afternoon. The ball had just come to him. It was almost an open goal and he was just about to kick it straight into the net when he stopped. The ball rolled past and the defenders took it back up the field.

"What did you do that for?" Craig yelled in his ear. "Open goal, you couldn't miss. Whose side are you on?"

"It was because of that man standing in front of the goal," said Dan without thinking.

Craig glanced briefly towards the goalmouth before running after the ball.

"You're nuts," he said.

Dan looked again. There was no man. The white-haired old man in the brown suit and open overcoat was not there any more. But he had been!

He was on his way home, by himself because he needed to be alone to think, when he saw him again, this time walking with a stick. The figure was somehow looking older now. It was time he put the whole affair to the test. Dan walked straight up to him. If he found he was making a mistake, he could always say something like, "Have you got the right time, please?"

"Afternoon, Mr Farrel," said a woman walking briskly towards both of them from the other direction. "Trouble with your leg, have you?"

"Just a touch of rheumatism," said the old man. "I'll survive."

"That's right," replied the woman, nodding to Dan as she walked on.

This man was real enough. He turned towards Dan and smiled that same smile.

"You're coming to me, now. You won't escape," the old man said quietly. "They never do."

He said it in such a matter-of-fact way that Dan was startled. What did he mean by *They never do*?

"I'm nearing the end of my time," the old man was saying, "and I need another body. This time I've chosen yours."

"What do you mean?" asked Dan, fearfully.

"I've had this body sixty-one years almost to the day. It's getting old."

Dan had his mouth open in horror. The old man was staring at him fixedly, almost as if trying to see right inside him. There was no doubt he really meant it.

"Who are you?" Dan asked in terror.

"My name is Charlie Farrel. And before that it was Albert Howe. And before that Henry Fix ... And my next name will be yours."

Then Charlie Farrel limped off. He had not walked with a stick before, Dan thought as he hurried after him. He was really scared now!

"What do you mean?" he called. One or two other people on the pavement turned and stared, but he took no notice of them. There was something he needed to know.

The old man stopped again, still with that evil smile.

"Work it out for yourself," Charlie Farrel said very quietly. He was standing so close that Dan could smell his foul breath. "Years ago, I discovered how not to die. Since then, I never have. I am able to select someone of the right age and become that person. Then when that body grows old ..."

He leaned forward until his face was almost touching Dan's. He spoke earnestly now, and the smile was gone.

"You won't feel any pain," he said. "I shall just take you over at a time when you are conscious but not able to resist."

Dan had heard stupid stories of people being possessed by devils and evil spirits, or whatever, but had never believed a word of it. Now this old man was claiming that he was going to possess him! He looked around at the bright, sunlit afternoon and it all seemed unreal.

So Charlie Farrel was going to take him over when he was conscious but not able to resist, eh? Did that mean Mr Farrel was powerless while he was asleep? Was that why the cold hand kept waking him up? Was the idea to weaken his resistance through lack of sleep, so that very soon he would no longer be able to stop this dreadful creature?

There was no doubt that Dan was in the grip of something really evil, but exactly what, he didn't yet understand. The only certainty was that Charlie Farrel might succeed unless he found some way of escape.

If he was telling the truth, of course. There was one way to find out that might give him some help. He had been Charlie Farrel for sixty-one years – so he said. But he looked well into his seventies. Suppose, sixty-one years ago, he really had taken over a boy of about his age named Charlie Farrel ...

The next day was Saturday. During the night, the apparition had appeared twice. By the morning, Dan was worn out through lack of sleep. He was sure that was the plan now, to lower his resistance until the inevitable happened. Tired or not, though, Dan just had to do what he had planned.

He caught the bus into town and arrived at the offices of the *Herald*, the local weekly paper. When people died, they printed their names in the deaths columns, didn't they?

"Yes?" asked the woman behind the counter.

"Is it possible to look at copies of your newspaper from sixty-one years ago?" Dan asked hopefully. "It's for ... er ... something we're dong at school."

Established 1874 it boasted over the

doorway of the newspaper offices. So they should be able to manage something from only sixty-one years ago.

"You can look right back to the first issue, if you like," said the woman amiably. "Come into the back." She opened the counter flap and invited him in.

He expected to find a room filled with piles of old newspapers, or at least lots of big folders with them inside. Instead she looked along the shelves and took what looked like a cassette tape from a little box.

"It's all on micro-cassette nowadays," she said. "Here, I'll show you how to work the machine.

She inserted the cassette, switched it on and left him to it. On the tape was the entire newspaper, every page for the year. Dan wound it along until he found the week he was looking for.

Most of the notices in the obituaries column were fairly short, but he suddenly found a much longer one for Albert Howe. There was no mention of a Charlie Farrel, but then it struck him.

Of course, Charlie Farrel hadn't died as far as anyone knew. He would have been taken over, intact, by Albert Howe. There was much more about Albert Howe on the second page, when he turned the tape back. Mr Howe, former Mayor of the town, had died suddenly at the weekend. There in front of him was a photograph of Mr Albert Howe. It was same man who was haunting him now! But this was sixty-one years ago!

Now what was that other name? ... Fix ... Henry Fix ... He read on because he needed to know. Mr Howe had been seventy-five at the time of his death, just about the present age of Charlie Farrel. So somewhere between about fifty and sixty years before, Henry Fix would have died if Charlie Farrel had told him the truth.

Dan looked up at the shelves and found the micro-cassettes of the paper for those years, took them down and slipped them all through the machine. It didn't take long now he knew exactly what he was looking for.

He found it in the year 1886. Mr Henry Fix, well-known general dealer, whose shop at 35 Church Street ... there was no photograph this time, of course. But Dan would like to bet that if there had been one it would have shown the same face as that of Henry Howe, the same face as Charlie Farrel had now.

This creature took over the body of someone much younger than himself. Then lived the life of that body until it grew old when it left it and took over another body. As it grew older, it seemed clear that this body took on the appearance of the living vampire who occupied it.

A terror seized him at this thought. How long had this been happening? How many times had the man now calling himself Charlie Farrel taken over a young body and started his life again? It could have been going on for centuries!

The panic died down. He had to think of a way out of this mess, some way of breaking the chain. There was only one solution, but the problem was how to make it happen. The woman behind the counter was astonished when the boy walked out without even thanking her, but Dan had things, other than good manners, on his mind at the time.

He caught the bus back, but instead of going home, he hung about the streets, working it out. The man would be somewhere about. He obviously knew all about Dan and where he went during the week. Possible he didn't know what he might be doing at a weekend. He hoped not, because he knew now what he had to do, whatever the consequences.

It was nearly one o'clock, and not many people were about. Most were either at home, having done their Saturday shopping, or had not yet started out. Then he saw him near the bus stop. There was no mistaking the figure with the walking-stick, already leaning on it more heavily than he had the day before. It seemed that he had not much time left.

Dan retreated round a corner and waited until he saw a bus coming towards the bus stop. At that moment, he began to run towards the old man, faster and faster, and finally bumped into him as heavily as he could.

The old man uttered a cry as his stick flew out of his hand. He struggled to save himself, but failed. His body went in front of the bus and he was shunted along the road several metres before the bus could pull up.

The driver climbed out, shaken.

"I'll ring for an ambulance," said Dan, setting off for the nearest phone box.

He took a long time getting there and a long time before dialling. After giving the details as slowly as he could he walked calmly back.

"I think he's had it," a man in the little group of people was saying.

Dan looked down at the crumpled body of Charlie Farrel. It was not moving. He looked dead, all right.

Dan felt very tired for the rest of the day. He went to bed early to try to catch up on some of his lost sleep. At least, he had no need to worry now. If Charlie Farrel was dead, he wouldn't be able to change bodies any more. The chain was broken at last.

He was just beginning to doze off when he was aware that he was not alone. The usual figure was standing there.

"There's not much time left," he heard, dimly. "Just lie still and relax. You're sleepy, aren't you? But not really asleep."

The figure was climbing on to the bed alongside him.

"Give me your hands. This won't hurt."

Dan could smell the same foul breath he had noticed when Charlie Farrel had spoken to him in the street. Cold hands were searching for an opening between the sheets and moving down the bed.

Limply, Dan tried to move those hands away. He could feel the cold moving over him as the ghostly fingers crept round him. His senses were beginning to go. There was a kind of blackness stealing over him, as if the world was starting to fade away. He could struggle no longer.

So this was how the creature had done it all those years before! A cold chill was striking through him, a darkness surrounding him, deeper than the blackness of the night. He fought against it ... weakly. This time he knew he was going to lose. In a matter of minutes, Dan would be gone.

"I haven't much time," the voice was muttering, not from a distance now, but right in his ear. "The surgeon is operating."

A sudden change came over the apparition just as Dan had started to thrash about in the bed in a final effort to resist.

"No, no!" Charlie Farrel cried loudly, and seemed to stop moving suddenly. He flung himself upon the terrified Dan ... and vanished!

Dan lay quite still for a moment, wondering if the change had taken place after all, but he still felt the same. He ran his hands over his body, trying to find out. Suddenly, he felt completely wide awake.

His mother was in the room with him.

"Another bad dream?" she asked, anxiously. "I heard you shouting."

"No, no, it's all right," he said. He hadn't been shouting. The apparition really had been there, if his mother had heard it as well. "It's all right now."

He fell asleep almost at once.

Next morning he had to make sure. He nipped out to the telephone box and rang the hospital.

"I'm enquiring about Mr Charles Farrel," he said. "He was in a road accident yesterday, about one o'clock."

"I'm very sorry," said the voice at the other end of the line, "but Mr Farrel died at half-past ten last night. Are you a relative?"

Dan replaced the receiver. No doubt he would be reading the details in the *Herald* later in the week.

The only thing was, how many more like Charlie Farrel were around waiting for boys like him?

THE DOOR IN THE WALL

S ophie sensed there was something odd the moment she began to walk along Warren Lane. She had a sudden feeling there were people around her and she even began to look for them.

Of course there were people in the street, but this was different. It was as if there were other people there apart from those she could see.

Then she found the green door in the wall. It was an ordinary wooden door that she had never noticed there before. What was more, it lay invitingly open. Since she was in no hurry, she peered through and then stepped inside, feeling sure there ought to be a large garden on the other side, which was strange, since it was supposed to be a building site!

They were clearing the area to build a new apartment block. Part of it was already completed at one end of the large open space.

Now this was very odd indeed. From inside, the apartment block was not visible at all. Perhaps it was behind the tall trees at the far end of the garden. It seemed a great shame to destroy a beautiful garden like this to build apartments on.

There was a huge house standing there, too. It had a semi-circular path running round to the door from the main entrance on the other side, and an ornate fountain playing in the middle of the lawn.

Sophie sauntered along the narrow pathway which led from the green door in the wall towards the house. If it was all going to be demolished anyway, nobody would mind her being in there, would they?

In fact, she was wrong. Just as she reached the front of the house, a lady appeared from round the corner wearing a long dress and carrying a white parasol.

"Oh, sorry," said Sophie, thinking she must have accidentally stepped in front of some television cameras. She looked round carefully and decided there were no cameras. Perhaps this actress was taking a walk between scenes.

"Why, Sophie," said the lady, surprisingly. "What have you to apologise for? Have you been doing something you shouldn't?" Then she smiled.

"No, I was just wandering and looking," said Sophie in great confusion.

"That's right," said the lady, smiling again. She entered the house and the door closed behind her.

This was puzzling. Sophie had never seen this lady before in her life, yet she knew her name. Perhaps she was confusing her with someone else.

She was going to be late, she thought, looking at her wrist to check the time. But her watch had disappeared! It would be terrible if she had dropped it somewhere. But she remembered she had been wearing it as she came through the door in the wall, so it must have fallen somewhere along the path. She retraced her steps, searching the ground carefully.

She had still not found the watch by the time she reached the wall, so she hoped it had come off on the other side and that nobody on the street had made off with it. She stepped out on to the pavement and began to look. Then she noticed it was still on her wrist!

When she turned round the door was shut firmly against her. She pushed it, but it seemed to be locked. Still puzzled she went home. She decided that on her way home from school, she'd return to the garden and try to get to the bottom of it all. It seemed a harmless enough adventure – just strange, very strange!

Her chance came the following day. Sophie usually caught the bus to school, but whenever the weather was fine she liked to walk home. It saved money, which was important now her father was out of work.

There was the door, open as on the previous day, so she stepped through it. Yes! There was the same garden, and the same house. This time, though, she paid particular attention to what happened to herself.

Her watch was the first thing to disappear. It didn't so much vanish as cease to exist. Then her skirt seemed to lengthen until it just cleared the ground as she walked forwards. Yesterday, she hadn't bothered to look at her clothes. She had just thought they felt different from usual.

She stopped this time to take stock of what was happening. She was no longer dressed at all, as she had been before entering the hidden garden. Now she was wearing clothes which she had only seen in photographs of Edwardian ladies in history books.

She was certain what had happened – she had fallen asleep and was dreaming. Perhaps she had sat against a tree and dozed off. The only trouble with that idea was that it didn't feel like a dream. There was no dream-like quality about it at all. Everything seemed very real and solid.

She touched one of the tall trees, then slapped her hand against it to make sure. She felt the hard bark against her palm and, when she looked, a faint red patch was appearing on her hand.

There was an old man coming towards her.

"You've returned!" he said delightedly. "And you're quite right, it's time we painted rings on those trees to keep the insects from climbing them. I will instruct the gardeners. Trust you to keep us on our toes, eh, Sophie?"

There was no time to explain that this was not why she had touched the tree. The old man escorted her towards the house, led the way up the five stone steps to the front door, opened it and held it wide for her. She had no real option but to enter in front of him.

"Welcome home, Miss Sophie," said a housemaid.

Well, she assumed she was a housemaid because of the way she was dressed – in black, with a neat white apron and a kind of cap on her head, rather like an old-fashioned waitress. The housemaid made a slight curtsey. Then a tall man in dark clothes and white gloves approached. He nodded his head towards her, almost in respect.

"Welcome home indeed, Miss Sophie," he said. "Granger, show Miss Sophie to her room."

At once, the housemaid began to walk up the wide staircase and Sophie, wondering whether she was doing the right thing, followed her along a long passage at the top of the stairs to a large door. The maid opened the door and stood aside.

"I'll have your luggage brought up, Miss Sophie," she said, and left her alone.

This was much more disturbing than wandering about in the mysterious garden. The room was a bedroom with wide windows overlooking the front of the house and the garden. From there she could see the pathway curving round towards a large entrance gate in the distance, with stone pillars on either side, and in front of her the fountain spilling water from a bowl in the hands of a statue into a pool below.

Against one wall was a series of doors, so she ran across and flung them open. Inside were dresses and gowns, the likes of which she had never seen before. She closed the doors again quickly. What was worrying was that now she was actually inside this grand house, she might never be able to escape to her own world again. Much as she fancied the life she was obviously expected to live here, she would not like to have to remain here forever.

That thought frightened her. But who was the real Sophie, and where had she been? Why had the old man, the maid and the butler all welcomed her back?

She had to escape before it was too late. When she opened the door, there was no one outside, so she hurried along the passage and down the staircase. Once at the front door, she opened it quietly, and leaving it open, ran into the fresh air. That smelt real enough.

She hurried along the little path between the trees towards the green door. Once through that, she knew she would be safe. She could always return the next day. These people she had met were obviously kind and meant her no harm. Far from it, in fact, for they had greeted her as if they were delighted she was among them.

Thankfully, she could see the door was still open. She didn't stop running until she was on the pavement outside and clearly back in modern times. She paused for a moment, out of breath, to check that she was back to normal herself, and her watch told her she had been on the other side of that door for not more than twenty minutes.

When she turned to look, the door was shut again, just as it had been the day before.

This was unbelievable! She could imagine what her mother would say about making up stories like that. Her father would only smile disbelievingly and say that if she happened to find herself smothered in diamonds next time, bring some back with her so he could sell them.

There was one thing she could do before she went home. The workmen had finished for the day, so the half-built apartment block would be deserted. She knew the stairs had been put in at least up to the second floor because she'd seen them. She squeezed through the fencing and climbed inside the new building. Then, from a gap in the wall where a window would be fixed before long, she looked out in the direction of that magnificent house and garden.

She was not surprised to find that there was nothing there – just a derelict area.

The next day was Saturday, so no school. She was determined to get to the bottom of her strange experience once and for all. So, in the morning, she deliberately walked along Warren Lane. The green door stood invitingly open, as she had expected. This time, she knew exactly what was going to happen – and it did. The only difference was that now her clothes were black. She walked briskly up to the house.

An open carriage with two horses in front of it was standing outside the door. Beside it was the woman she had seen the first time she had been there. She looked older, somehow, and was also dressed in black, with a black veil over her face. More carriages were lined up behind it. As Sophie watched, four men in black moved down the steps from the door carrying a coffin.

"Come, Sophie," said the lady, very kindly. "It is time we were off."

A footman lowered a step from the first carriage, and she and the veiled lady climbed in.

"Lower your veil," instructed the lady as the footman replaced the step and closed the carriage door. Sophie found that she, too, had a veil, and lowered it over her face.

The coachman turned round.

"Ready, my lady?" he asked.

The lady inclined her head slightly, and the carriages began to move from the house, along the driveway and through the large gates into the road outside.

It was silly to expect that out in the streets, she would see anyone she knew. Still, she looked anxiously at the people lining the pavements in case there was a face she could recognise. One or two seemed vaguely familiar, but that was all. They all stood in silence, the men with their hats in their hands.

Even the road was different. In fact there was nothing she could identify at all until the carriage turned a final corner and St

Stephen's church stood straight ahead. That was exactly as she knew it.

Suddenly, she understood. There was only one answer. This was the funeral of the old man she had spoken to only the afternoon before. Time somehow must have moved very quickly. That would explain why in two days, the lady beside her had grown old.

The carriage came to a stop, the footman alighted from the back, opened the door and lowered the step. Sophie stepped out onto the pavement and held out a hand to help the lady to get down. She wondered what was going to happen now.

What did happen was that the church remained unchanged, but everything else underwent an immediate transformation! Lorries were rumbling along the road, cars had stopped at the traffic lights, crowds were entering, leaving or passing the shops near the church. Her clothes were once more what she had been wearing when she had left home that morning. Yet she was standing outside St Stephen's church, with no logical explanation of how she got there. And no one seemed to have noticed the slightest thing strange!

She ran, dodging the crowds on the pavements, tripping over shopping trolleys which women were pulling behind them. She was in a desperate hurry to return to the house and garden she had left such a short time before.

Then she slowed down to consider her position and recover her breath. The question was whether to try to find the main gates of this strange house and march straight up to it, or whether to return to Warren Lane and enter through the green door – if it was still open, that was.

She chose the green door. At least she knew that if she went through there, she was sure of the change taking place. Eventually, she would be able to discover what this was all about and why it should be happening to her, of all people.

She took a deep breath as the door in the high wall came into sight. It was open! She hesitated for a moment, then walked boldly towards the house. Only as she reached the flight of stone steps, she paused to discover what she was wearing this time – a shorter dress to just below her knees, covered by a coat of the same length with a fur collar, and on her head a round hat with a feather sticking out of it.

She put up a hand to feel the feather. Then she felt a string of beads round her neck – pearls, without a doubt. The wristwatch had disappeared again, and on her hands were a pair of white kid gloves.

She stopped to admire an open-topped car parked in the driveway, gleaming and shiny as if it had come from a motor museum. She'd never even heard of a Napier car before.

The butler, much older now, greeted her at the door.

"I trust you enjoyed Le Touquet, my lady?" Then he leaned forward and muttered, much more quietly, "Things have changed during your absence abroad, my lady. I think you ought to know."

A youngish man brushed past the butler.

"Thank you, Bates," he said, abruptly.

The butler paused for a moment before bowing politely and withdrawing into the house. Behind him, Sophie could see a group of people of about the same age as the man who stood regarding her coolly. The man put an arm out to stop her from entering, then gripped her by the elbow and escorted her back down the flight of steps.

"You are no longer welcome here," he said fiercely.

Sophie was surprised, to say the least. She knew that time speeded up in this garden. It seemed to have begun in Edwardian days, but now it had clearly moved to the 1920s. She wondered if she was now the same age as this man who had such a tight grip of her arm, but without a mirror she had no way of finding out. He must have been about thirty, she supposed.

"So you can just clear off," he was saying, "and go back to your friends on the continent – or to the Devil, for all I care!"

"Who are you?" Sophie asked, coldly.

"Pretending not to know your own husband now, are you? Let me tell you, Sophie, that now as your cousin I've married you and inherited the estate as well as the title, I have what I wanted. The point is, have you got what you wanted?" He moved towards the house. "Bates!" he snapped.

At once the butler appeared.

"Kindly escort my wife from the premises."

"I would rather not, my lord," replied the butler.

"Then I'll do it myself." And he seized her arm again.

"Let go of me, or I'll sock you one," said Sophie belligerently. She was not the timid type, and besides, he was hurting her.

"Talking like a guttersnipe now, are you?"

Then came a swift slap across her face. First this took her by surprise. Then she became angry. She struck back hard, right on the end of his rather pointed nose, and was delighted to see him fall over backwards. His head struck the edge of the bottom step and he lay still.

Sophie stormed off towards the green door in the wall. What did it matter, anyway?

These people didn't really exist. She could do as she liked. She hurried through the door and stepped out briskly into the street.

At first she decided never to go into the garden again. But she wanted to know what the result of hitting that hateful man had been. She was a little scared, though. What if they took her into the house and kept her there?

It was several days before she found herself peering cautiously through the door, which was open again. She decided to risk it.

To her surprise, she was wearing the same clothes as the last time. Time had hardly changed, then. That somehow seemed ominous. She made sure she left the door open behind her in case she had to make a run for it.

Not so briskly now, she stepped up to the house and stopped. It seemed the entire household were on the steps. There was Bates, the butler; the maid she had seen once before, much older now; a dumpy woman in an apron who might have been the cook; another woman, more smartly dressed, perhaps the housekeeper or something; two men in uniform who might have been footmen; and right at the back a couple of girls of about her real age who were probably kitchen-maids.

The butler stepped forward.

"Congratulations on your acquittal,

my lady," he said. "Sir Geoffrey is waiting for you in the library."

Acquittal? She wasn't sure what that meant exactly, but thought it was something to do with being found not guilty of a crime. They glanced at where her supposed husband had been lying when she had left the last time. Then she knew. She had killed him!

"Lead the way," she said. She thought that sounded better than asking where the library was, because of course she had no idea. "And thank you all," she said to everyone. She knew that would have been expected.

Sir Geoffrey turned out to be a grey-haired man in a smart suit. He was standing at the library window as she came in, and on the table nearby a pile of papers were spread out. He came up to her and shook her hand warmly.

"As I told you at the outset, no jury would ever find you guilty of murder. Unfortunately, the death of that scoundrel of a husband has left you with many problems."

Sophie wondered what she ought to do. Now what would Lady Sophie do in these circumstances? She decided simply to sit in the nearest heavily upholstered chair.

"What problems?" she asked, trying to act as the real Lady Sophie might have done.

"The estate is in considerable debt, Lady Warren."

That was a shock, calling her by her own surname.

"Your late husband's extravagance and gambling have not only wiped out the entire estate, but left you owing a great deal of money. And, of course, the trial cost you many thousands of pounds. The only answer, I'm afraid, is to sell the house and the land. Now it so happens ..."

It became clear to Sophie at once. Next time, the green door wouldn't be there any more. Or if it were, it would not be open. This was going to be her final visit to the past.

" ... that the local council are interested in buying it. There will be some money left over, but certainly not enough for you to live in the way you are used to. But you have no other choice. You must sell."

Sir Geoffrey held out a large sheet of paper.

"As your legal adviser, I must ask you to sign where I have marked." He unscrewed the cap of a fountain pen and held that out to her as well.

Sophie signed the paper with her own name.

"I won't touch a penny of Henry's money," she found herself saying. Then she wondered how his name had suddenly come into her thoughts. She hadn't known it before.

"But you must," said Geoffrey. "Otherwise, how will you live?"

"I'll manage," declared Sophie, grimly. This Lord Warren must have been a right berk, she thought to herself, as well as a right nasty piece of work.

"At least claim the surplus money from the council," urged Sir Geoffrey.

"Not on your life!" said Sophie, haughtily.

"Then I shall place it in an account in your name –"

It made no difference what he did, Sophie was thinking. As soon as she went out of the garden, everything would disappear anyway, just as these clothes she was wearing always turned back into her own.

She flung the pen down and swept out, out of the house, down the five stone steps, across the driveway and on to the narrow path between the trees, and out through the green door and into the street. She was enjoying herself. Just like being an actress in the last scene of a television play.

Outside on the pavement, when everything was back to normal, she stopped to think. She looked back. The wall was solid now. There was not even a green door in it, only a bricked-up outline where one might have been, years ago. She hurried off home.

"Dad," she said, "why is our name

Warren?"

Her father laughed.

"What do you want to be called, Smelly?"

"No – I mean, we're called Warren, and there's a Warren Lane, isn't there? Have there always been Warrens in this town?"

"Who's been talking to you about it?" asked her father, sharply.

Sophie had been trying to work it out all the way home. Lady Warren had been alive in the 1920s, when she had killed her husband by accident. She was suddenly feeling excited. That could make Lady Warren her great-grandmother!

"What happened to great-grandma?" she burst out.

"So somebody *has* been talking," said her father, "haven't they?"

The suspicion resolved itself at once. She had been her own great-grandmother! But something still didn't make sense. The name would have changed by now. It wouldn't still be Warren.

"Your great-grandmother went to live in Canada after a little scandal she was mixed up in. That's where her son, your grandfather, was born. When she died, he returned to live here. And that's how we come to be here. Now – why do you want to know?"

"What happened to the money?"

"What money?"

"What was left over after the estate was sold. We did own that land where they're building the apartment block, didn't we?"

Her mother came in from the kitchen.

"The Warrens owned almost half the town in their day," she said. "But there's no point in harking back to that now, is there? Imagine what people would say if they knew your father was one of the Warrens. Why, we'd be a laughing stock!"

"Why aren't you Lord and Lady Warren, then?"

Both her parents began to laugh.

"Because nobody could be sure that your great-grandmother's son was the son of Lord Warren or one of the old girl's many boyfriends instead, that's why! Your grandfather never claimed the title. There was no point. There was nothing to go with it anyway, so the title came to an end."

Her mother seemed amused, but Sophie wasn't.

"All right," she said, "if you can prove that Lady Warren *was* my great-grandmother, the council owes us some money. They've got to give it to us, haven't they?"

"How do you know all this?" asked her father, quietly.

"I dreamt it," replied Sophie, quickly. "At least, I think that must have been it."

"I'll look into it," promised her father. "Tomorrow, after I've been to sign on for benefit, I'll pop round to the council offices and ask. But I'm telling you, there won't be anything in it for us. Things just don't work out that way."

This is virtually the end of the story. The extra money left over might not have amounted to much in the 1920s, but by the time interest had been added for all those years, Mr Warren found he'd never have to worry about money again! They were even able to move house.

As for the wall in which the green door had appeared – even that had gone now. One day, Sophie was walking along Warren Lane to find it had been demolished so they could complete the building of the apartment block.

Warren Court was the name given to it. Sophie was quite proud of that. She knew that her great-grandmother would have been pleased, had she been alive to know anything about it.

Perhaps her great-grandmother was alive ... second time round ... so to speak.

Other titles available in the *SCARUMS* series ...

	ISBN	COVER PRICE
Noises In The Night	1 84161 031 3	£2.99
Sleep Well	1 84161 030 5	£2.99
The Ghost Train	1 84161 032 1	£2.99

Available from all good bookshops, or direct from the publisher. Please send a cheque or postal order for the cover price of the book/s, made payable to 'Ravette Publishing Ltd' and allow the following for postage and packing ...

UK & BFPO	50p for the first book & 30p per book thereafter
Europe & Eire	£1.00 for the first book & 50p per book thereafter
rest of the world	£1.80 for the first book & 80p per book thereafter

RAVETTE PUBLISHING LTD
Unit 3, Tristar Centre, Star Road, Partridge Green,
West Sussex RH13 8RA